The door opened and Hawk came in first, and three steps behind him was Jaggers. Slocum's hand went back and the knife flashed through the air, buried itself in Hawk's chest. Slocum held Hawk's body in front of him, pulling Hawk's gun from its holster, bringing it up. Jaggers had his gun out, and fired, hitting Hawk. Slocum fired and his bullet struck Jaggers' forehead and he went staggering back as if he'd been poleaxed. He fell against the wall.

Slocum poured the coffee into a tin cup, not even looking at the two dead men. The coffee was hot. He liked the taste of it. He took another deep breath.

Dawson—it was one helluva town.

OTHER BOOKS BY JAKE LOGAN

SIX-GUN BRIDE

BERKLEY BOOKS, NEW YORK

SIX-GUN BRIDE

A Berkley Book/published by arrangement with
the author

PRINTING HISTORY
Berkley edition/December 1985

ISBN: 0-425-08392-6

A BERKLEY BOOK ® TM 757,375
Berkley Books are published by Berkley Publishing Group,
200 Madison Avenue, New York, N.Y. 10016.
The name "BERKLEY" and the stylized "B" with design are trademarks
belonging to Berkley Publishing Corporation.

PRINTED IN THE UNITED STATES OF AMERICA

SIX-GUN
BRIDE

1

The young woman was peaches and cream, and her curly red hair danced as she moved on the hot dirt street. Slocum, walking his roan to the nearby saloon, looked with pleasure at her. He'd been riding dusty trails toward Dawson for a week, and until now he hadn't fixed his eye on a pretty female form. The redhead glanced at him, a lean, bronzed, square-faced rider sitting tall in the saddle, and she didn't see the cowboy backing out of the saloon. He was obviously drunk. They collided and, because the cowboy was unsteady, he went sprawling in the dust.

He sputtered curses and lay for a moment staring at the girl, who, though jolted, was unharmed.

"Why'n hell don't yuh look where yuh goin'?" he snarled.

Slocum, who had expected the cowboy to make a

graceful apology, scowled at the boorish remark. The cowboy was well-dressed in a tailored black shirt, cord pants, a black Stetson. He had a narrow face, small dark eyes, and the look of a spoiled brat.

The girl, a spirited filly, said, "You backed into me, mister, and if you weren't drunk as an owl, you'd not be down there."

He scowled, still down in the dirt. "Smart-alecky filly, aren't you? Bumpin' a man, knockin' him down, then callin' him drunk. Who'n hell are you?"

She glared. "I don't know who you are, mister, but you sound like an ornery polecat whose manners need mendin'."

The cowboy flushed and stared hard at her. Then, becoming aware of how pretty she was, he licked his lips.

"Made a mistake, miss. I'm sorry. Now if you jest give me a hand gettin' up, I'd be content."

She wondered if she'd been wrong about him. Then, because she was young, lovely, and happy, she decided to pass over his loutish words, and reached out her hand.

He took it, lifted himself, then grabbed her close. "Tell yuh what, missy, I'll forgive and forget if you gimme a nice, juicy kiss."

She pushed at his chest. "I'd rather kiss a rattlesnake."

Slocum, now nearby, swung off his horse. He'd been grated at the cowboy's bad manners. A yearling spoiled rotten, who needed a hard lesson and fast.

Stung by her remark, the cowboy struggled to pull her close, and she slapped his face. Thereupon, he slapped her face.

Slocum stepped over, grabbed the arm holding the girl, and twisted it hard so that the cowboy released the girl. Then, with a short right, Slocum hit the cowboy's jaw and he went down. He lay there, a bit stunned.

"Not much of a gentleman, are you, cowboy?" Slocum's voice was mocking.

The cowboy's dark eyes blazed with fury, and he grabbed at his gun. Slocum shot it from his hand.

It didn't seem to faze the cowboy. Slowly he got to his feet, his face dark with anger. "You don't know who you're messin' with, mister."

Slocum stared into the rage-filled eyes and laughed. "If you don't start moving, little cowboy, I'll put you 'cross my knee and whip the tar outa you. Now git."

The cowboy glanced at the men who'd come out of the saloon and were watching. Fearful he might be humiliated again by this lean, powerful stranger, the cowboy, his face surly, leaned over to pick up his hat. He put it on his head and studied Slocum. Then he smiled a strange, secret, mean smile. He had control of himself now. He threw a look of contempt at the girl and swaggered off.

Slocum watched the cowboy, aware that such a man was not to be trusted. But he didn't look back, just swung over his mustang and rode up the street.

"Thank you, mister," said the redhead.

"The name's John Slocum, and it was a pleasure, miss."

She had a pert nose, a wide mouth, cornflower-blue eyes, and freckles. "Doreen," she said. "I suppose I was partly at fault. I wasn't looking."

"A lady's never at fault," Slocum said.

"I'm new in town. S'pose I shoulda been a bit more polite. After all, it was him on the dirt. But he acted so uppity, like he was the big noise in town."

"He is," said a red-faced old-timer who had been sitting on a chair in front of the saloon and who had obviously seen it all. "He's Rusty Hogarth. And his father, Luke Hogarth, is the biggest rancher in Dawson." Then, under his breath, he muttered, "And Rusty is the meanest brat in Texas."

"Are you stayin' in Dawson, Mr. Slocum, or just ridin' through?" Doreen asked.

"I aim to stop here to draw breath. Been riding the trail for a week."

"Well, it's a pleasure to have a red-blooded man like you in town. Makes a body feel protected." She blinked her eyes at him and flounced toward Cutter's General Store.

"That's Doreen Smith. She's seventeen actin' like twenty-two," said the old-timer.

Slocum's face fell. A springtime bud, and he was aching for a grown-up woman.

Just then the saloon doors swung open, and about six men came out, cold-eyed, bulky, grim-looking men mostly dressed in dark, tight-fitting jeans and shirts. Slocum, with his experience, judged them to be gunfighters or hired guns. They didn't laugh, didn't swagger, just looked cold-blooded and businesslike. They seemed to have something on their minds and, after an icy, curious look at Slocum, they swung over their horses and galloped west out of town.

Slocum tied the roan to the railing and went into Bryan's Saloon. The men at the bar looked at him and he saw nothing cordial, more fear than anything else.

A stubble-bearded cowboy at the end of the bar smiled, and Slocum took a place beside him.

A craggy-faced barkeep called Sal hobbled over, a gleam of humor in his dark brown eyes. "What's your poison, cowboy?"

"Whiskey, my friend. Your best."

Sal cocked an eyebrow. "Got one brand here, cowboy, and it curls your hair."

Slocum grinned. "As long as I survive."

Sal put the whiskey bottle on the counter with a glass and Slocum drank two quick shots to cut the dust.

The liquor burned, and he felt a slow loosening. He'd been riding the trail for more than a week, and he was saddle-sore and needed a stopover.

Behind the bar hung a roughly printed sign: DANCE AT BIG MILLAR'S BARN TONIGHT.

"Where'd you ride in from, mister?" asked the stubble-bearded man, smiling.

"John Slocum's the name. Came off the trail riding west."

"Higgins is my handle. You sure pulled a fast gun out there." Slocum looked at Higgins. He had light blue eyes and a sandy complexion and looked friendly enough.

"Who was that brat cowboy?" Slocum asked.

"The meanest of them all. The Hogarth polecat. Rusty. The old man is the cattle baron in these parts. He's a fine old man."

Slocum nodded. So he had tangled with the pup of the big bull in Dawson. Well, it didn't mean a thing to him. He'd loaf here a couple of days, then ride on. Too bad the red-headed filly was so young. He might do better at the barn dance. He talked for a time with Higgins about the trail. Then the saloon doors swung open and a lean, dark-eyed, black-shirted cowboy stood there, looking calmly at the men at the bar. The heavy silence made Slocum glance at the man. He was fitted in tight Levi's, a tight black shirt, black hat, and slickly polished gun handle. Everything about him spelled gunfighter. His black button eyes were fastened on Slocum. Then he walked easily on scuffed brown boots to the bar and took a place about eight feet from Slocum.

The men gave him space, and it clearly had to do with the threat of his presence.

Slocum went on talking casually to Higgins. He sensed the gunfighter's interest in him, but he couldn't figure out the reason.

"Gimme whiskey," the gunman said, his voice flat.

The barkeep nodded, poured a drink, and left the whiskey bottle. "Hot day, Bullitt."

Bullitt just nodded, emptied the glass, poured another, emptied it. Then he hefted his belt, leaned on the bar, and watched Slocum.

"What do you do for fun in this town?" Slocum asked Higgins, totally ignoring the gunfighter.

"They got some good-lookin' lassies in town, Slocum. You could do worse than go to the dance at Millar's Barn tonight."

"Might take a look-in," said Slocum.

"Look in where, Slocum?" asked Bullitt.

Slocum turned slowly. The gunfighter's black button eyes were staring insolently and his small white teeth glittered through his partly open lips.

A crawly polecat, Slocum thought, who had come

out of the woodwork and was looking for trouble. Was it aimed at him, he wondered? And why?

"I figured there might be something to do at this dance." Slocum's tone was friendly.

The button eyes just stared. It was a dead look, with no feeling. "No, not for you, Slocum."

Slocum turned his body so he was clear of the bar. "Why not, mister?"

The gunfighter's body was already turned to Slocum, and it was taut. "I got a feelin' you ain't gonna make that dance tonight." His mouth took on an ugly twist.

Slocum's jaw hardened. This miserable hyena who made his living doing executions for whoever paid him was itching for a fight. Slocum couldn't for the moment figure any good reason. But there was no avoiding him, and he was probably a fast gun.

"You aim to stop me?" Slocum asked.

The men nearby had been edging back, and at these words they flattened against the wall.

"Yeah, see, mister, I don't like the look of you. You remind me of 'Tallman' Kelly, a polecat I been trying to nail for a long time. For all I know, you may be him."

Slocum, who watched the button eyes like a hawk, saw them suddenly narrow, and, as he talked, Bullitt had his gun coming up. Slocum's pistol coughed, and the gunman looked jolted, astonished, then slid slowly to the floor, trying to bring his gun up. He fell, firing into the floor.

Slocum shook his head. He knew that gunfighter trick of talking calmly at you while he went for his gun. It hadn't fooled him yet.

The men at the bar looked relaxed for the first time. Some even smiled at Slocum.

Higgins came close.

"Why'd he do it?" asked Slocum.

"That's the way they do it," Higgins said. "He was Jack Bullitt, one of the gunmen who's been poisoning this town lately. There's been killin's of good upright citizens. We need a fast gun like yours to help clean 'em out."

Slocum shrugged, poured a drink, and gulped it. "I'm not here for fighting, Higgins. Gonna loosen up, then I'm gone."

He didn't even glance at the dead gunfighter as he walked out the door.

At the Dawson Hotel, he rented a room, locked the door, and lay down on the bed for a couple of hours. When he awoke, he took a bath and shaved. He felt hungry as a bear. He stopped at Lucy's Home-Cooked Meals, ate a thick steak, corn, black-eyed peas, candied yams, coffee, and a double helping of pecan pie.

After that he felt on top of the world. He stepped into the night, smiling and at peace, when a grinning cowboy with shoulders big as a barn door came from behind him and swung a haymaker that if Slocum hadn't moved by instinct would have torn his head off. Even so, he was jarred to his toes and sat down, looking dazedly at the monster cowboy who leaned down, pulled Slocum's gun, and threw it thirty feet away.

"What the hell did you hit me for?" Slocum managed to croak.

The cowboy looked anxious. "You're Slocum, aren't you?"

Slocum nodded slowly, an act of pain.

The big gorilla grinned good-naturedly. "That's why I did it. I'm Bullhead Stevens, and I'm here to break your back."

Slocum brought his hand to his head. Bullhead was about six foot five, weighed about 280 pounds, and his biceps were big as thighs. He didn't wear a gun. He didn't have to. He was waiting for Slocum to get up.

"I got no beef with you, Bullhead. Think you made a mistake," Slocum said hopefully. He could never take this monster out with his fists.

"No mistake, Slocum. You're my meat. So get up. I'll put you to sleep fast. I got some chores to take care of." He cocked his fists and waited.

"Couldn't you take care of your chores first, Bullhead?" Slocum suggested politely. His eyes frantically searched the area.

It was a quiet time, the dinner hour, and there was scarcely anyone nearby. What kind of town was this? You mind your own business, but people shoot at you and knock you on your tail.

"Get up, get up, or I'm goin' to be forced to hit a man when's he's down. Which I don't mind doin' in your case, Slocum."

Slocum got to his knees, facing sideways from the big man who, he had noted, in spite of his great muscles, looked soft in the middle. He made a sudden rush, butting his head at the man's gut.

There was a grunt as Bullhead, too clumsy to move, stood his ground. Slocum fell back. It was like hitting a stone wall.

"That was not nice," Bullhead grumbled. "Guess I'm gonna have to tear you to pieces, Slocum." He

made a grab for Slocum's arm and flung him head-
first at the standing wooden column. If Slocum hadn't
managed to swerve, his head would have cracked open
like a melon. He missed it by a quarter of an inch,
but his arm felt as if it had been stung by a hundred
needles. The big man lumbered toward Slocum as he
frantically scanned the area. He was near an aban-
doned well which worked by cranking with a thick
wooden pole slotted into an iron holder. Bullhead was
coming on like a freight train and Slocum, aware that
he could be snuffed out once those bear arms caught
him in a clutch, moved fast, rolling just out of the
reach of Bullhead, who lumbered past. With a quick
move, Slocum reached for the pole and pulled it with
a prayer. It came loose. Not waiting for Bullhead to
turn, Slocum sprung after him, swung the pole at the
back of his skull. There was a dull thunk and, to
Slocum's horror, Bullhead turned as if some flea had
swatted him, gazed at Slocum, grinned comically, and
took a step. Then all at once his eyes spun crazily,
his legs melted, and he dropped. He put a hand under
his head, shifted his body as if to get comfortable,
and went to sleep on the ground.

Slocum looked at the mountain of muscle lying
there, then went for his gun, which glittered in the
moonlight. When he had it he dropped the pole.

Slowly he felt his body for broken bones, then
made a beeline for Bryan's Saloon, where he quickly
drank two shots. Some drinkers, remembering his early
encounter with Bullitt, grinned. He tried to grin
back, but it hurt. He checked the damage. His body
felt bruised, his left arm mangled, his jaw was stiff;
otherwise, all his organs were intact. That was some-

thing to be grateful for. Bullhead Stevens was a destruction machine and Slocum had survived only because he never let Bullhead get a firm grip.

Where had the monster come from? And Bullitt? Men were coming out of the woodwork to attack him. Why? He had stopped in Dawson for a breather, and all he had met was mayhem. This was one tough town. Was this Rusty Hogarth's doing? Did that spoiled brat send a man like Bullitt to do his dirty work? Or a gorilla like Bullhead? You'd hardly think they would pay attention to a miserable brat like Rusty. But, according to that cowboy at the bar, Higgins, Rusty was the son of a big cattleman, Luke Hogarth. That might give him plenty of muscle. But would the father permit it? Someone had called Luke Hogarth the pillar of the town. It was odd. He'd have to keep an eye out for Rusty.

Music from the outside drifted into the saloon, and his eye went up to the sign behind the bar. That was what he needed, a fun place and a fun filly to help ease his hurts. He might have to rest his weary body before he'd be ready for dancing. He smoked and sipped his whiskey.

2

As they neared her house, a mile out of town, Marylou stepped in front of Slocum. The silver moon, which flooded the silent land with light, sharply outlined her buxom figure. Slocum, his blood humming with the whiskey he'd been drinking at the bar and the dance, threw an appreciative eye at her well-formed buttocks that moved with sexy rhythm under the thin blue dress. *She's all honey and curves,* Slocum thought, *and the promise of good bedtime fun.*

He couldn't help feeling a quiver of pride in the way that Marylou had fastened on him, favoring him above all the cowboys at the dance. She had fluttered her violet eyes at him, sidled up wearing that silky blue dress that could hardly hold the swelling flesh of her breasts. Naturally, he danced with her. One word led to another and the last to an invitation to her

13

place and a furthering of their friendship.

Slocum, whose loins were charged with lust, deprived as he had been of women during his long ride into Dawson, looked at the sexy Marylou as a gift from heaven.

He was a bit astonished, he had to admit, at the hot and heavy way Marylou had thrown her body at him, but he put it down to her good taste.

He moved behind her with his graceful, catlike walk. His scuffed boots were quiet on the silent earth. His piercing green eyes raked the nearby land. Habits of caution were a major reason for Slocum's survival in dangerous territory. Even now, when nothing more than a night of sexy fun appeared to be ahead, some deep, primitive instinct sent him uneasy signals.

But they were drowned in the stampede of feelings that started from the moment he stepped inside her house. For she pressed her voluptuous breasts against him, and the warmth of her thighs set his flesh on fire, especially when she put her soft mouth against his and her hand went boldly down to his erected flesh and started vigorously caressing.

My lucky day after all, he was thinking when she suddenly disengaged and lit the lamp, which sent a warm amber glow through the room. There was a wooden table, a dresser with a bottle of whiskey and glasses, a wide, low bed with a yellow coverlet. Through the back window, the light of the moon silvered the trees and bushes behind the house.

"I feel like another whiskey, Slocum," she said.

That surprised him, because he figured that she, like him, was caught up in excitement.

"And I feel like a lot of hugging," he said.

"All in good time, Slocum," she said, and shifted her heavy breasts.

He poured two drinks and she smiled brightly at him as she sipped her glass. "So you are John Slocum."

"Been calling myself that long as I can remember."

She crossed her legs, as if she was in the mood for talking. "I'll tell you a strange thing. I knew a man who took the name of Billy the Kid, just for the glory. Happened not long ago. This young cowboy came through here, like you, and said he was Billy the Kid. Naturally, one of our ambitious boys figured he'd make a name and demanded a showdown." She studied him. "What d'ye suppose happened?"

Slocum scowled. Why in hell was she babbling like this after starting a fire in his britches? He didn't like it.

Marylou glanced at him, and her mouth was a hard line. "I see you're dyin' to know, so I'll tell you. This fellow who claimed to be Billy sneaked outa town so fast he looked like greased lightning. See, there's a lot of fakes out there, claiming to be somebody big till the chips are down."

He looked at her breasts, her mouth, and wondered what in hell her game was. "The name's Slocum. And I guess you brought me here on false pretenses. So let's call it a night." He stood up.

She frowned, startled by his words. "No, don't go." With a quick move, she pulled at her dress and stood in front of him stark naked.

This is more like it, he thought. He drained his glass, pulled off his clothes, and his male flesh pranced out, swollen and eager.

Her eyes glistened. "That's a man-sized thing you got there."

He laughed. "'Stead of admirin' it, whyn't you make its acquaintance, Marylou?"

"Ah, yes." She looked around the room, out the window, as if wanting to make sure everything was all right. Then she came close to him, took hold of his flesh in a petal-soft hand, and pressed her lips against his mouth. He felt her heavy breasts against his chest and put his hand over the smooth, silky flesh, touching the nipple. His other hand went down between her legs and his finger entered the wet warmth. He stroked her, then leaned down to touch his tongue to her nipple. She sighed, yielding to the pleasure. Then she suddenly sank to her knees to his swollen flesh and put her lips against it. As if caught in a gust of passion, she took him into the warmth of her mouth. Her movements were slow and expert. When he felt the sharp rise of excitement, he brought her to the bed and turned her, holding her firm, rounded buttocks. He slipped between them to her soft wetness and began to plunge in and out, enjoying the flow of sensations. He turned her again, and she lay on the bed spreading her legs, and he went into her hard, and began a thrusting that reached her. She let loose a long, drawn-out groan. His rhythm became strong and she picked it up, and he felt a great flow of sensation as his tension kept rising until the final surge, and her body shuddered when he climaxed.

Then she went silent.

"That was great, Marylou," he said, rolling off her.

She still said nothing, which surprised him, for he could tell her body had gone through the raptures. He

shrugged. There was something odd about her anyway. She seemed to be enjoying the sex even though
she didn't really want to. As if something in her was
fighting it. *To hell with it,* he thought. His own pres-
sures were nicely wiped out, and he felt drowsy. In
the excitement of sex, he completely forgot his hurts.
Sex surely cures a man of his pain, he thought, and
he soon dropped into a deep sleep.

He didn't know how deep into the night it was, but
he came suddenly awake, though his eyes were closed,
alerted by his instinct for danger, an instinct that seemed
always to recognize that something nearby had about
it the threat of death. His eyes didn't open fully; he
just listened. He couldn't hear breathing, and Marylou
no longer lay alongside him, but someone was in the
room. Someone was trying to move silently toward
him. His muscles tensed. No sound, but a pressure in
the air of something moving closer. Closer.

Then the silver moonlight silhouetted Marylou and
glinted off the knife in her fist, raised to strike. Her
arm started down and he caught her wrist, turned it
hard. She groaned and let the knife fall. His glance
swept the room. Empty. Why did he think someone
else was there?

"Lemme go," she whispered through clenched teeth.

He flung her on the bed, scooped the knife off the
floor, then slipped on his jeans, belt, and gun. Naked,
he felt too vulnerable.

She was wearing a housecoat. She lay there staring
at him more in frustration than fear. He lit the lamp,
then a havana; she was watching him with hostile
eyes. He almost laughed. She had just tried to stab

him, and now she looked outraged that he had stopped her. He sat on the bed beside her and shook his head. "You got a funny way of being grateful for my love-making ways, Marylou."

She threw a venomous look. "It's not your lovin' ways. It's your *killin'* ways, John Slocum."

"Nobody's trying any killing here but you."

"You done yours," she snarled. She tried to rise, but he held her wrist. "Lemme go," she said.

"You ain't goin' anywhere. Now, who'm I s'posed to have killed?"

She glared. "You know. Don't play dumb with me."

He stared. Was it possible that Marylou had some connection to a low-down gunman like Bullitt? "What's this about? Now tell me."

She glared but said nothing. He put pressure on her wrist.

"You polecat," she gasped.

"Just tell me."

She glared. "You shot my kin, that's what you did. Cold-blooded murder."

He scowled. "Cold-blooded murder? Jack Bullitt was your kin?"

"I'm not talking about him," she snarled. "To hell with you."

"Tell me, and be quick." He twisted her arm.

"All right, all right," she groaned.

He leaned to her, and the knife fell from his belt. As he bent to scoop it off the floor, a shot crashed through the window, and Marylou's eyes glazed suddenly and she dropped.

Slocum threw himself to the floor as another shot whistled past his head and crashed against the wall.

His own gun was out, and he fired without a target. All he could see was the soft gleam of moonlight, the trunk of a tree, and dark shadows. He couldn't risk a movement to the lamp, for it would make him visible. He stayed flat, glanced at Marylou. The bullet had hit her head and she lay glassy-eyed. He bit his lip, threw a shot outside. If he put out the lamp, he could get to the window, and once there he might be able to pick off the gunman. He crawled toward the lamp. Another shot blasted the window and hit the wall. He was pinned down. He waited a moment, then shot out the lamp. The dark gave him security. When his eyes adjusted to the dark, he began a slow crawl to the window. Outside all was quiet except for the crickets which turned up their volume. It would be dangerous to prowl about in the dark; he would wait till the crack of dawn. What about Marylou? Someone had shot her just when she started to talk. Why? To keep her mouth shut? And someone wanted him dead. This was one hell of a town.

At the crack of light he would pick up the tracks and find out what was what. As for Marylou, he would bury her, then track and catch the killer. In territory like this, the only law was the gun.

When dawn streaked, he peered through the window, his eyes raking the land. Nothing. He came out cautiously. The gunman had left tracks. The gunman had lurked behind the thick trunk of the tree and peered into the window; after he fired, he had thrown himself on the ground and crawled back. He had fired again from a farther tree, as powder marks showed. The gunman's horse had been tied thirty yards back. He had ridden west.

Slocum's jaw hardened. This polecat was out to

kill. He had killed Marylou to keep her silent, and Slocum, too, was the target of that gun. The sooner he tracked down this gunman the better.

The tracks moved toward high ground, land that was pockmarked with ravines, hills, and boulders. As the tracks went over the hard, rocky ground, Slocum studied every boulder that could hide a gunman.

Three hours later, he found a campfire where the gunman had stopped to eat; the ashes were still warm. His eyes raked the area. Up ahead there were four places from where a man, if he were holed up, could shoot. It would be dangerous to prowl in the clearing. He would linger here and try to draw fire, just in case. He had reason to believe the gunman was no sharp-shooter; otherwise Slocum would be dead back in Marylou's hut.

So he moved around, managing always to be near cover. But nothing happened, and he had just come to the conclusion that the gunman had moved on when a pistol roared and the boulder next to him chipped pieces. He hit the ground and crawled behind the boulder for cover. The shot, he felt, came from a flat-sided boulder out a hundred yards, and he fired at it to pin the gunman down.

Now it was a matter of circling, coming behind this polecat, and smoking him out. He threw bullets at the flat-sided boulder to keep his man nailed down, then he began to crawl flat down, moving from cover to cover, until it was safe to come up to a crouch. Silent as an Indian, he skirted the rocks, working a wide circle, peering out when he felt it right, to make sure his man did not make a run.

It didn't take long before he came in sight of the

gunman, crouched behind the rock, peering out, in a puzzle about what his tracker was up to.

Slocum smiled: he'd find out in a minute. Silently he moved to within thirty feet of the gunman, then stepped out, gun ready, and spoke in a clipped tone. "Drop the gun or you're dead."

The man froze, dropped his gun, and turned.

Slocum stared.

It was a woman in jeans, vest, and Stetson. He came forward, his mouth clamped. What in hell was happening to him in Dawson? He seemed to be everyone's target, men and women.

The young woman was staring at him with such hatred in her pretty brown eyes that he kept his gun handy.

"Who the hell are you? And why did you shoot Marylou?"

Her mouth pressed hard, her eyes just blazed with hatred. She said nothing for a full minute. Then, "Are you going to kill me, too?"

"It's *you* who killed Marylou. Why? And why'd you shoot at me?" he asked.

"'Cause I want you dead," she rasped, then bent to tie her shoe. Instead she grabbed a rock, threw it at him, and started with surprising speed toward her horse, which was tethered to a tree in the distance.

Though he had ducked, the rock struck his shoulder, and he cursed as he went after her. A flying tackle brought her down and they tangled on the ground. She clawed at his face, trying for his eyes.

She hates the hell out of me, he thought as he smothered her body with his and pinned her arms. She breathed heavily, her breasts rising and falling.

Looking at her closely, he was struck by her beauty. Her skin was clear as a lily, her eyes flashing brown jewels, her lips full and well-shaped, and her hair, now that it was free of her Stetson, glowed like gold. Her body was curvy and firm under him. Why did such a beautiful woman feel so much venom for him? What in hell was happening?

"Are you gonna rape me?" she gasped.

He had to laugh. "You sure got some funny ideas about me. Expect me to kill you, rape you. Who the hell are you?"

She stared coldly. "I'm Cassie Gaines, that's who I am." Her voice was accusing, as if her name should mean something to him.

"Cassie Gaines. Am I s'posed to know you?"

"Know me! You shot my father. And you won't get away with it."

He scowled. "Shot your father? Gaines? Never met the man. I'm sorry your father's dead."

Her lip curled with scorn. "Wouldn't expect a killer to admit his crime."

"You saw me do the shooting?" he asked.

She hesitated. "There's plenty of witnesses saw you. Cold-blooded murder."

It was the same phrase Marylou had used. "Why'd you shoot Marylou?"

Her face distorted with pain. "I was shootin' for you, and you ducked down just at the wrong moment!"

He drew a deep breath. Both of them out to get him for a killing he didn't do.

"If I let you up, promise you won't run. I won't hurt you. I swear it."

She said nothing. She didn't trust him.

"Who are the witnesses who claim I shot your father? Name one."

She glared. "Rusty Hogarth and the men with him. They saw you. You're one of the gunmen killing ranchers in Dawson."

Slocum's jaw hardened. He had to get this Hogarth off his back if it was the last thing he ever did. "Rusty Hogarth," he said, "is the biggest liar in Texas, Miss Gaines. I never met your father. I don't shoot in cold blood." He leaned forward. "I whipped Rusty for assaulting a girl in front of the saloon. Since then he's been trying to get me, one way or another. I'm gonna track him down and wring the truth outa him."

She stared at him, as if, for the first time, there could be a crack in her belief that he had killed her father.

"Who was the girl?"

"Doreen is the name she gave."

"Don't know any Doreen," she said, her eyes narrowing with suspicion.

"She's new in town, she said. Find her. She'll tell you." He got up. "You're mistaken about me, miss. I figure you got a lot of grievances. I have some, too. I'm gonna get fast hold of Rusty Hogarth if it's the last thing I do." He turned to her. "Who is Marylou to you?"

She stood up. "My cousin. She heard your name at the dance, sent me a message that she'd bring you to her home. No time to get help. I came myself. Too late. I tried to get you. I'll never forgive myself for Marylou." Her head sank on her chest. "In one day I lost my father and my cousin." Her eyes were filled with tears.

He bit his lip and moved close to her, put his arm on her shoulder to give human comfort.

At first, she was too overcome by grief to resist. Then she pushed him away, her face fierce. "I don't know yet if you're a liar. Just let me go."

He moved back. "You always could go. You'll be hearing from me, Cassie Gaines."

He watched her walk toward her horse, a lovely young woman, holding her hat, her head bent in sadness. The sun caught her hair and it glowed like burnished gold.

Slocum's jaw hardened. Yes, this was one hell of a town. Rusty Hogarth was not only a spoiled brat, but a rotten liar. And his father was the biggest bull in Dawson. He had a feeling it was not going to be easy to put a lasso around Rusty Hogarth.

3

Slocum decided to make coffee before starting back. It might pay for him to think for a while about what had happened since he hit this misbegotten town. He poured the bubbling coffee from the pot into his tin cup and sprawled against a partly sunken rock. While sipping, he looked at the land. It was lush and summer green and, to the west, the great Sierras climbed with solid grandeur. The clouds were great cotton tufts that hung without movement against a cobalt-blue sky.

He thought about Cassie Gaines, a beautiful golden-haired filly with lots of guts. She had gone bold as a lion after the man she believed had shot her father. But she seemed to have more guts than brains, taking the word of a man like Rusty Hogarth.

This Rusty was a polecat who had to be nailed. A liar down to his boots, he had sworn, as Slocum remembered grimly, that Slocum had killed Cassie's father. Witnesses, too. Who could they be but some of his people? A poisonous brat, this Rusty. Because he had been knocked down in front of people, he nursed a vicious grudge.

And he was dangerous. How could you explain why a gunman and a gorilla of a cowboy should, out of the blue, let loose with gun and fist? Rusty Hogarth had to be behind that. And he didn't waste a minute with idle threat. He just tapped a couple of desperadoes and they came down on Slocum like a ton of iron. He might be young, but he was dangerous as a rattler. More dangerous, because he didn't rattle before he struck.

As Slocum sipped his coffee he thought of Higgins. He had said, "There are gunmen in this town killin' the citizens."

At the time Slocum hadn't paid attention, because he hadn't reckoned on being in town long. Now he felt differently. He wanted to clear himself in the eyes of Cassie Gaines. He didn't intend to let a nasty pipsqueak like Rusty Hogarth get away with a false accusation. And he wanted to find out if Rusty was the man sending out those ornery characters.

Slocum thought about the gunmen. What could they be after? Most gunmen, unless they were plain loco, didn't kill except for hope of gain, sometimes because of insult. Something was going on in this little Texas town, and it might be interesting to get to the bottom of it. He would look around, and he might have to clear up the killing of Bill Gaines to clear himself.

Most of all he felt a strong pull to help a beautiful

girl like Cassie Gaines, who was going through a bad time.

He emptied his cup. Time to go to town.

As he walked toward the roan, he told himself to stay extra sharp. In a town like this, you didn't know who was going to hit at you.

On the trail back he had to climb a ridge which gave a long, circular view. The neigh of a horse drifted up, and looking down he saw a young woman, nude, flouncing in a flowing stream. Her well-shaped breasts jiggled as she jumped. Her hair, long and black, hung wetly about her white shoulders. She was enjoying herself, and Slocum felt a touch guilty as he continued to watch her. When the young woman became aware of the powerfully built cowboy on the fine horse watching her, it didn't seem to bother her. She walked calmly to the bank where her clothing lay. At the sight of her body, Slocum felt like whistling: the slender waist widening to voluptuous hips, the dark hair that nestled between her finely shaped thighs and legs. She began to towel herself, bending her torso gracefully as she shook water out of her hair.

Slocum sat like a statue on his horse. Then, smiling, he nudged his roan along the trail.

To his surprise, the girl stopped toweling and stared directly at him. He couldn't tell if she was accusing him or inviting him. She had to be one brazen maiden, unfrightened of man or beast. As he rode along, he wondered who she could be, but soon he began to think of how he could lay hands on Rusty Hogarth.

As he rode down Main Street in town, he saw a small knot of cowboys in front of the saloon surrounding a fallen man. It had to be a shooting, Slocum thought. That's where the whiskey fired the blood, and the fracas started. A wrong word, a mean look, a slight bump—and first the words would fly, then the lead. He swung off the roan and walked closer. A well-dressed cattleman lay on the ground, his chest soaked in blood. A grey-haired old-timer was bringing a buckboard alongside.

Slocum spoke to the slender, red-faced cowboy next to him. "Who was he?"

"Sam Walker." There was recognition in the blue eyes of the cowboy. "Sam owned the Bar W ranch. A fine man."

"Who shot him?"

"A gunman. Came into the bar, had a few drinks, turned nasty, and picked on Sam. 'Bout nothin'."

Slocum looked at the dead cattleman, a strong-looking man about forty. "Why'd Walker pull his gun?"

"Forced to. Insults. But it was cold-blooded killin'."

Slocum took a havana from his shirt pocket and lit it.

"You're Slocum," the cowboy said. "Saw you hit Rusty Hogarth. Beautiful sight."

Slocum nodded and watched two men lift the body and put it in back of the buckboard. He had started toward the hotel when he heard a familiar voice behind him.

"Mind if I join you?" It was Higgins, his stubble-bearded face grim as he watched the buckboard drive off. "They're taking him home to Rachel Walker. A rotten job."

They walked silently up the street. Then Higgins

said, "The man who killed Sam was a gunfighter. Must be a way of avoiding a fight with a man like that."

"Hard to think of one."

"This town has gone bad," said Higgins. "It's the gunmen. They kill, then go off west. Don't know where they hole up. Dunno why they're killin'. It's not like anyone's getting robbed. It's just mean, pointless shootin'."

"Most shooting's like that," Slocum said. But this was one hard town, he was thinking. Dawson had a mean bunch, and he wondered if one of them had knocked off Bill Gaines. Now why in hell did Rusty Hogarth swear Slocum had killed Cassie Gaines's father? That was a mischief. The girl said there were witnesses. What witnesses?

"Why don't the men here do something to clean up things? This Luke Hogarth seems to be a big honcho. What about him?" Slocum looked at Higgins.

"Luke Hogarth is a four-ace man, right-minded. He's done good things for this town. For people in trouble. A fine gentleman. But he won't go for vigilante action. Thinks it's dangerous. The wrong man might get killed."

"What about this Rusty? A mean varmint, seems like."

"That's it. Hogarth ain't blessed by his kids. Rusty is spoiled rotten. Can't understand how he got sired by a man like Luke Hogarth. Then there's Lulabelle, a wild filly. It's sure a pity, 'cause you'd never want to meet a nicer man than Luke Hogarth."

Slocum thought about the girl he'd seen bathing. "What's this Lulabelle look like?"

"A beauty. Lines of a thoroughbred. She goes after what she wants. Nobody can put a bridle on Lulabelle Hogarth."

She sounded like the girl he'd seen naked. He thought of her sexy body, the way she looked at him, and damned if he didn't get a tingle in his loins.

"Do you know Cassie Gaines?" Slocum asked.

"Sure. A sweetheart of a girl. Lost her dad, I heard. Too bad."

Slocum stopped walking and looked at Higgins. "She came after me. Thought it was me that shot her father."

Higgins stared. "You? Shot Bill Gaines? Sounds crazy. Why'd she think that?"

"She says Rusty Hogarth saw me."

Higgins whistled. "Rusty. I'll be damned." He chewed his lip. "Well, did you?"

Slocum's eyes narrowed.

It jolted Higgins. "Of course you didn't," he said hastily. "It's a crazy idea. That Rusty is a mischief maker. It's 'cause you rubbed his nose in the dirt. That's why he said it."

"Where can I find this polecat?"

Higgins rubbed his chin. "You could go out to the Hogarth ranch, on the trail west. Or wait till he comes to the saloon. He has a taste for liquor."

When they reached the hotel, Higgins said, "Sure wish you'd use your gun on this nest of snakes. They've spoiled our town."

"There's one snake I'm interested in. Rusty Hogarth." Slocum went into the hotel.

He lay on the bed in his room with his hands behind his head, staring out the window. He could see billowing white clouds in a dark blue sky. His eyes felt heavy and the lids slipped down. Images swirled in his drowsy brain. A woman's figure turned toward him, gun in hand. Golden-haired Cassie. She raised the gun, pointed it at him. He put his hand up and, to his amazement, stopped the bullet. Felt no pain.

She looked furious. "Why'd you shoot?" he asked. "Because you shot my father," she said. He grabbed her gun and she slapped his face. He pulled her tightly to him, kissed her. She looked stunned, then raised her face, kissed him, and began to unbutton her shirt. He felt the hardening of his flesh. Then his eyes opened on his hotel room.

He could see through the window that the clouds had shifted and were spread thin. He'd been sleeping for quite a time, and his dream was idiotic.

He dashed water from the basin over his face, clattered downstairs, and started up the street. His boots kicked up small puffs of dust as he walked through the rows of ramshackle houses.

He had the barbershop at the other end of town in mind. Jovial voices floated out to him from the saloon up ahead. Then he noted two men leaning against the railing on the porch of the saloon. They were bulky and broad-shouldered, and wore brown vests, blue jeans and red neck bandannas. They were watching him.

Slocum walked slowly, his senses alert. He had no idea who they were or what they would do, but they looked like men who handled guns. In this town you didn't know from moment to moment if someone would throw a bullet or a fist at you.

As he neared the saloon, they moved out in front of him. One man smiled, showing plenty of teeth. He looked ready to enjoy whatever was about to happen.

Slocum bent at the waist, his green eyes narrowed.

Now he could see their faces, one broad-boned with a thick pudding nose and small red eyes, the other with a lined face and lantern jaw.

The man with the lantern jaw spoke first. "Whyn't you ask this cowboy, Jed? Looks like he might know somethin'."

"Mebbe you're right, Burt. Looks like a know-it-all." The small red eyes stared at him insolently. "Say, mister. We're lookin' for a man called Slocum. Happen to know where we can find him?"

Slocum looked at them. A bad situation: two men, gunslingers—he'd met too many not to know.

"Why are you lookin' for him, may I ask?" he said.

"Shore you kin ask. Right, Burt? We hear he shot Bill Gaines. And we'd like to pay him our respects."

Slocum's jaw hardened. It was a setup. They were playing a game. They knew who he was. And maybe they knew who shot Gaines. He would play a game of his own.

"I know Slocum, and I'm telling you he never shot Gaines. Can I ask who told you he did?"

The saloon bat-wing doors swung over, and a man peered out. Then he came through the doors to the porch, followed by four other men who'd come to watch slaughter on Main Street.

Jed and Burt were looking at each other. "Sounds like you know a lot, mister. And that you're doubtin' our word."

"Just want to know who told you *he* shot Gaines."

"What's your handle, mister?" Burt asked, his small mouth twisting in his long face.

Slocum's face was a mask. They figured they had him, because they were two. But they were close together, close enough; he needed every edge he could get.

"Slocum's the name. And I didn't shoot Gaines."

Nobody on the porch moved, as if the scent of death had come up strong. "Wouldn't expect you to admit it," Burt said.

The pulse was beating strongly in Jed's forehead. "Rusty Hogarth told us, and his word is good enough for me."

"Rusty Hogarth," Slocum said, "is a pipsqueak liar. And it will be a bad day for him when we meet again."

"But you're not goin' to meet him," said Jed with a mirthless grin.

To the men on the porch the next moment was a dazzling display of movement as the two pistol shots came so close they sounded like one. The two men hurtled back as if kicked by mules, blood spouting from their chests. Jed fired into the ground as he sank to his knees. Burt cleared his holster, but his gun never fired. Both men fell slowly on their backs and lay still as the glaze of death came over their eyes.

Slocum looked at them with a face of granite. He had figured Jed would be the fast one. Slocum hated to think what would have happened if he had shot at Burt first and given Jed an extra pulsebeat of time.

Because the barber shop was situated at the other end of town, and someone was playing a harmonica, nobody in the shop heard the shooting.

The barber, a bald, grey-eyed man with a nicely trimmed mustache and beard, looked up from the man whose hair he was cutting, and froze at the sight of Slocum when he opened the door.

"Bust my britches," he said, "if it ain't Captain John Slocum in the flesh."

Slocum grinned. It was Sergeant Joe Hawkins, who had ridden with him briefly in the Quantrill days.

"Hawkins, you're a sight for sore eyes."

"What in hell are you doin' in a hellhole like Dawson?"

"Hopin' to pass through it unharmed. But not if I put myself in that barber chair. Still hackin' hair like a butcher, Hawkins?"

Hawkins laughed. "Mighty dangerous talk for a man 'bout to set under my razor."

The dignified grey-haired man in the chair smiled.

The barber turned to the man whose hair he was cutting. "This is Captain John Slocum of the Georgia Regulars. Deadliest rifleman they ever put up against the bluecoats. If we had more men like him, we'd never've lost the War. Rode with Quantrill, too."

The grey-haired man turned to look at him and smiled. He had penetrating grey eyes and a strong, ruddy face, and his smile was gentle. "This is Mr. Luke Hogarth," said Hawkins. "He owns the Bar H ranch. If you decide to stick in Dawson, Slocum, Mr. Hogarth is the man to talk to."

So this was the father of Rusty. Not quite what he expected.

"It was a bad thing for us to lose the War," Hogarth said in a deep, musical voice. "It left a scar that won't go away. It's destroyed a way of life, a gallant way of life. And we can't ever go back to that again. It's a pity. It's a new world. A hard world." He stood up from the chair and looked at the mirror. "You give a good haircut, Hawkins. Surprised that your friend called you a hacker. Seems to have a sense of humor." His piercing grey eyes measured Slocum as he put out a strong hand. "I'm always interested in good men. If you decide to stay in Dawson, ride out to my ranch. Be delighted to offer you work you'd like." He smiled gently and went through the door.

Slocum sat in the barber chair. "So that's Luke Hogarth."

Hawkins nodded as he threw a towel around Slocum's neck. "Richest man in these parts. Owns about forty thousand head of cattle and thousands of acres. A mightly generous man. Helps people."

"Owns a mean son, too."

Hawkins looked grim. "Rusty? He's on the wild side, but smart. Hogarth lets that boy run free. So you found Rusty out, Slocum? How?"

"Little run-in at the saloon." Slocum's voice was noncommittal.

Hawkins grinned. "A little run-in, he says. We all know what Slocum means by a little run-in."

"Ever see any of the old bunch, Hawkins?" His voice was low. It was his way of talking about the Quantrill days.

"Naw. Most of them are shot up. Those who weren't, scattered. But Jesse goes through here sometimes. He's got folks out toward the river. He stops for a haircut and talks about the old days in Kansas. They were wild, weren't they, John?"

"Wild," Slocum agreed, his eyes somber. There had been a lot of blood spilled, and he didn't particularly care to think about those times. "All right,

Hawkins, cut away, and try to do as little damage as you can."

As Hawkins settled down to snip away at his hair, Slocum shut his eyes and remembered the old days with "Bloody" Bill Quantrill. They had killed his sister in prison. And Bill, too, died with a bullet in his chest, blazing with two pistols to the very end.

A cowboy with frowsy long hair came in, threw a sharp glance at Slocum, then sat down.

Hawkins gazed at him. "Here for your semi-annual haircut, Lorrie?"

"You're lucky I don't make it annual, Hawkins." He smiled at Slocum. "Hate to lose my hair, in case I run into a Comanche. Don't wanna leave him unsatisfied."

"This is Captain John Slocum, an old friend from the Quantrill days, Lorrie."

"Just seen the captain in action, Hawkins."

The barber stopped cutting. "What'd ya see, Lorrie?"

"Seen him cut down two hot gunmen with what sounded like one shot. Jed and Burt. They're planting 'em now in boot hill."

Hawkins stared at Slocum in the mirror and shook his head. "A couple of hyenas. They came here for haircuts. Guns for hire, I reckon."

"Why are they doing all this shooting?" Slocum asked sharply.

"Hyenas always are shootin'," said Hawkins. "This town has got a lot more dangerous in the last month. Killin's almost every day. Archie Brown, Bill Gaines, Lemuel Comstock, Sam Walker." Hawkins shook his head. "Dunno what's come over the folks. All this gunfightin'. Didn't used to be like this. Times have gotten bad." His scissor stopped clicking, and he looked at his handiwork with admiration. "Look at that, Slocum. The ole hand hasn't lost its cunning."

Slocum examined himself in the mirror, then smiled wryly. "The ole hand may not have lost its cunning, but it hasn't found it either."

He laughed at Hawkins's outraged face, clapped his shoulder, and reached into his pocket for a dollar. "It's okay. You're the best little barber in Dawson."

"West o' the Mississippi, you mean, Slocum." Hawkins looked balefully at Lorrie. "I been wantin' to put a guillotine to that head o' hair for months. Set your tail down."

Next morning, after bacon and eggs at Lucy's cafe, Slocum walked to Cutter's General Store to get tobacco. Blue-eyed Doreen, in a pink shirt and blue jeans, was looking at a pink bonnet.

"Well, there's John Slocum. Been wanting to thank you for your help. Dad was mighty pleased when I told him what happened."

"A pleasure, Miss Doreen."

She flounced a bit. "Just Doreen will do. How do you like this bonnet? Look silly on me?" She slipped it over her head.

"Nothing could look silly on you, Doreen."

She postured and flashed her eyes at him, and he took a deep breath. She might be a young filly, but she was all blossomed out, with a fine bosom and nice hips.

"I might just buy this bonnet because you like it."

He smiled. Young girls loved to flirt to test their

power over men. "Are you settled in now?"

"Oh, yes, we've settled in." She leaned to him, her voice low, though only Cutter, the proprietor, was in the store.

"You know that impudent drunk we had a fuss with? He's one of the Hogarths. They're the big shots in town, I hear. Guess I started on the wrong foot. But he acted like an ornery polecat."

"More like a rattler," Slocum said, thinking of the men sent against him. It had to be Rusty behind those unprovoked attacks. How else explain it? Just a hostile town where everyone was ready to slug anyone else?

She turned to Cutter, a slender, bald man with glasses and a smudged apron. "I'll take this bonnet, Mr. Cutter."

After Slocum got his cigars, they walked out together into the raw sunlight.

"I'm riding out to White Bird Creek, that's our place." Her lips curved in a flirtatious smile. "It wouldn't hurt to have an escort a lady could trust. Bad things have been happening in this town."

He stroked his chin. She was a young thing, but womanly, and sprightly as a spring flower. He liked the sunshine of her smile. And it was true that a mean bunch of hyenas hung around this town. Up to now there'd been no incidents with women, but it might happen.

Doreen swung over her Appaloosa. She looked good in the saddle, her breasts stuck out, her posture erect. He rode alongside her.

The air was balmy June and the trees and grass looked green and nourished. The mountains bulked with huge majesty against the burnished blue morning sky. They rode for almost half an hour until they reached a small stream where they stopped to let the horses drink.

Doreen swung off her horse, bent to the water, and drank from cupped hands. Her jeans pulled tightly about her shapely buttocks. Slocum took a deep breath. For a fledging, he told himself once again, she sure had a full woman's body. And there was no doubt that she was throwing signals at him. Maybe she was no lily of the valley.

She sat against the trunk of a cottonwood, pulled a weed, and brushed it against her smooth cheek.

"Whole town's talkin' about that shooting yesterday outside the saloon," she said.

He pulled a havana from his chest pocket and lit it. He was thinking about her innocence.

She smiled, perhaps aware of his thoughts. Females always sensed when you were feeling sexy, he thought.

"They're saying you're a good thing for the town," she went on.

He shrugged. "Just defending myself."

She shook her head. "You may be defending yourself, Slocum, but it's cleaning things up a bit. I heard tell there's a bunch of terrible men collected here in the last month. Bad killin's going on. For no reason, Dad says."

"Gotta be a reason," Slocum said. "Nobody but a loco kills without reason."

"The men have been talking about getting together to clean them out. But they're scared. These men are gunfighters, Dad says."

Slocum smoked and watched her thoughtfully.

Doreen's pretty face became serious. "I worry about Dad. Don't want him caught in any crossfire."

"Might be smart to keep your dad from coming into town for the time being, till this bunch goes elsewhere. Can't imagine what they want. Not all that much to steal around here." He looked at her. She was fresh as a daisy, with skin like a Georgia peach; her lips were finely cast and her rounded breasts pointed impudently at him. And she was flirting.

"Hard to believe you're so young, Doreen."

She scowled. "Who told you that?"

"Heard you were seventeen acting like twenty-two."

She flushed angrily. "Wish some ole folks would mind their business. Been eighteen for three months. And I know a thing or two. But if you think I'm an innocent little ninny, you can just mount your horse and ride off."

He bit his lip so that he wouldn't laugh. She seemed to be bragging about being wicked. She probably figured he wouldn't touch her if he thought her innocent. Was the old-timer on the porch wrong about her?

"All this time I been thinking you were pure as a lily."

She grimaced. "Didn't say I was a wicked hussy, either." She leaned toward him. "If I were, I s'pose that would interest a man like John Slocum, a man of the world."

"You like to play with fire, don't you, Doreen?"

"Fire warms a woman." She leaned closer to him.

He felt a tug of passion. Should he start a fire that couldn't be put out? He moved closer to her lips. "Are you a woman of experience, Doreen?"

Her smile was mysterious. "A man never knows

that until he tries to find out."

That did it. She might be a tender shoot, but her body was woman, and she wanted him. He bent and kissed her lips, which were like soft velvet. She put her arms around him. He could feel her firm breasts against his chest, and his flesh erected. She kept her lips pressed against him and he began to stroke her body. She had sensual curves, a slender waist, womanly hips, and rounded buttocks. She leaned back into the tall grass, lay there, held her arms out to him. He leaned over her, his hard male flesh pressing against the warmth of her loins. She drew a deep breath at the impact, aware of his bigness. Her lips parted and he kissed her, his hands stroking her breasts. He felt the pressure of her loins against him, and he reached beneath her shirt to the flesh of her breasts. They were round, firm, pink-nippled. His tongue was over one and she sighed, pulled him closer while her body strained against his. A woman of experience, after all, he thought.

"These clothes," he muttered. Within a minute they were both naked, and his eyes feasted on the look of her body, the slender waist widening to the strong curve of her hips, the billowed breasts, the well-moulded shape of her thighs and her pink peeping lips, modestly covered with brown fuzz. Her eyes were wide at the sight of his rigid maleness, and her hand went to it. And as he kissed her breasts, her body, she stroked him. She was a feast of youth and loveliness. His finger touched the pink lips between her thighs, and she sighed as he stroked, working into the juicy warmth. Not virginal, he was delighted to discover.

He slipped over her body and her thighs widened as he went into her. She was wet, marvelously tight, and she groaned with pleasure as he pierced deeper. She breathed his name, and her fingers gently clawed his back with her passion. He pushed until he was entirely within her, and her hips began to move with instinctive sureness. His fingers went behind her buttocks, curved and silky, and he worked in and out of her; she caught his rhythm, and there was intense pleasure in the tight pull of her. He enjoyed this for a time, then paused, let his hands caress her body, then started again, feeling, after a time, the soaring tension. Then, as his passion intensified, he began a frenzy of movements which caught her, and they moved with fierce rhythm which reached its climax as he swelled and exploded. A cry came from her, and her body coiled as great waves of pleasure surged through her. He felt marvelously drained.

She looked up at him, starry-eyed. "Not so innocent after all, John Slocum."

4

Later, after they had dressed and were almost ready to ride, she said, "You must come out and meet Dad. He admires you."

"I just may sometime," he said, and then he saw them, four men on horses, riding straight at the stream. Even from this distance they looked burly, all except Rusty Hogarth. It was a ticklish situation. He had the girl, and Rusty had three big cowboys, probably men from his ranch.

They rode directly to the stream, and swung off their saddles to let the horses drink.

Rusty walked toward them, followed by his men. Rusty didn't have his father's rugged look and never would. He had a narrow face with pale brown eyes, and a thin mouth pulled in a curl, as if he expected to find something rotten in the world.

Slocum, expecting something abusive, was astonished at his words. "Miss Doreen, I been looking for
you. Wantin' to apologize for my bad manners t'other
day. Guess I had too much whiskey."

Doreen, who had been scowling, looked surprised,
then pleased. "Glad to hear you say that. Many a good
man says the wrong thing when he's had a bit too
much."

Rusty smiled. "I get mean as a rattler when the
whiskey is in me and do the wrong thing. So again,
I ask your pardon."

She smiled broadly. "I'm more than happy to forget
it. And I think it's a fine thing for you to say this.
Nobody's perfect. Though I'm new in town, I heard
such fine things said about your father, that it did
make me wonder."

Rusty stared hard-faced at her for a moment, then
smiled. "Yeah, Pop's so damned perfect it's hard to
live up to him."

Slocum was still astonished. This didn't seem to
be the same spoiled brat he'd tangled with two days
ago. Was he wrong about Rusty? Whiskey did bring
out the mean streak in some men. But how could that
explain the gunfighter and the bruiser who had tackled
him so soon after he knocked Rusty down?

The pale brown eyes were gleaming. "I'm sorry,
mister, we had that run-in. You did the right thing."
He rubbed his chin. "Though I don't like to get hit.
It gets me overexcited."

Slocum nodded. This Rusty was turning out to be
a surprising character. Was this the real Rusty? Slocum
wondered if the father had said something. He sensed
a certain slyness in this man. But he could be wrong;

he'd made mistakes about people before.

"I'm glad you're taking it that way. Sorry I had to hit you. Couldn't think of another way to stop you."

Then Rusty smiled, and there was something so secretly wicked in it that Slocum's instinct for danger went alert.

Rusty rubbed his chin thoughtfully. "Nobody who hit a Hogarth ever lived to tell about it," he said cheerfully. "But I behaved bad." He hesitated. "And I heard tell of good things about you. The way you knocked down a coupla gunfightin' hyenas makin' trouble in our town."

The men behind Rusty listened quietly. Slocum glanced at them: hard-faced, burly men, clearly picked for brawn, and who knew for what else.

Again Rusty smiled. A real smiling man. "So everything's right between us, Slocum?"

"Almost everything."

Rusty's eyes narrowed and his face hardened.

Slocum hitched his belt. "There's this funny thing Cassie Gaines told me."

Rusty looked cagey, and his glance slipped casually to the cowboy on his left, a man with a pockmarked face and cold grey eyes.

"Cassie Gaines," Rusty drawled. "A beautiful girl. Didn't know you knew her, Slocum."

"Miss Cassie told me you saw me shoot her dad." Slocum's voice was easy. "Did you tell her that, Rusty?"

Rusty stared, and Slocum glimpsed the same devilish expression he'd seen when, knocked to the ground, Rusty pulled his gun to shoot at their first meeting.

But this time he had no whiskey in him, and had

better control. He took a few moments for thought.

"I'm sure surprised Cassie said that. I didn't say that *I* saw it. I said someone, a *stranger* did the shootin'. Then *someone else* said, 'Only stranger in town is Slocum, a big, lean cowboy, and could it be him?' *I* never said it was you. She got it scrambled up."

It sounded logical, but Slocum, staring into those pale brown eyes, felt that Rusty was lying. The only way to prove it would be to put Cassie and Rusty together. Well, Rusty had sure tried to clean up his character. Why was he at such pains?

Now Rusty backed away, smiling. "Dad tole us you rode with Quantrill, Slocum. That really hit me. Lotta people down here thought Quantrill was a hero."

Slocum was startled by the guttural curse that came from the man with the pockmarked face. He came forward, husky, muscled, taut as a piano string. He wore a black vest and a small black hat, and a cigarillo was clamped in his teeth.

The thong of his gun holster was up. A gunfighter ready for action, Slocum felt.

"So you rode with Quantrill, did you, Slocum?" The man's grey eyes were icy, and Slocum recognized a killer.

"I knew Quantrill," he said quietly.

The man showed his teeth and spoke slowly. "Then you knew the most rotten dog who ever lived."

Nobody moved or breathed.

"What's your name, mister?" Slocum's voice was cool.

"I'm Spotted Jack Smith. Quantrill killed my brother Johnny in Kansas."

"I'm sorry to hear that." Slocum's body was mobilized. It sounded like a plant, the whole thing. A hired killer, this Spotted Jack, out to do Rusty's dirty work? Maybe.

"You may be sorry, but you rode with that rotten dog, and that's enough for me." His gun was coming out as he talked.

"Hold it!" Slocum bit the words out, for in a lightning move, he had his own gun pointed at Smith's chest.

There was a freezing moment when Spotted Jack glared at Slocum, in shock that he'd been outdrawn, and was a hair's-breadth away from death.

"Put it back and live, Smith."

A slow smile crept over Smith's face. Carefully he slipped his gun back into its holster. Slocum, too, put his gun back. Doreen breathed a sigh of relief.

Smith turned as if to go, then wheeled sharply, his gun in hand, but Slocum's gun roared first and Smith reeled back and fell. Lying on his belly in agony, he raised his gun and pointed it at Slocum, but his vision blurred and, when he fired, the bullet went wild. His face fell to the ground and he lay stone dead.

Slocum, his green eyes like points of ice, turned to Rusty. He was staring at the dead man, then gazed at Slocum.

"Damn it, I never dreamed that Spotted Jack would pull a gun like that. Sure am sorry this thing happened, Slocum. Didn't know Spotted Jack had a brother killed in Kansas. Never would have talked about Quantrill." He shook his head. "Beats all hell." He turned to Doreen. "I'm sorry, Miss Doreen, that you had to see this bad thing." He motioned to his men "Take care of Smith. We'll give him a proper burial at the place."

The men, sullen-faced, slung Smith over his horse, and within minutes they were gone over a rise and out of sight.

Doreen's face was white. "A terrible thing to see. You gave him a chance to live."

He nodded and slipped a bullet into the empty chamber of his Colt. "Never seen a town like this. A lot of mean-spirited hyenas in this town, pulling their guns for no reason."

Her blue eyes looked puzzled. "He seemed to have a grievance."

"What grievance?"

"His brother. Didn't he say his brother was killed by the Quantrill men? And he figgered you rode with them."

"Maybe yes, maybe no. How do we know he even had a brother?"

She frowned. "What do you mean, Slocum?"

"Maybe all he wanted was an excuse for a shooting."

Her pretty face wrinkled with perplexity. "Why would he invent a story about his brother? Why would he want to shoot you?"

He smiled. "Since I've hit this town, I been forced to defend myself at least four times against men who seem to have nothing on their mind but to shoot me down or hammer me into the ground."

She frowned. "That's what Dad was talking about. These drifting gunfighters who have come here, and whose only sport seems to be shooting someone down."

He thought about it. Was he imagining that he was the target? It was true that other men also were shot at. Hawkins had named at least four. Because the attacks came after his run-in with Rusty, Slocum naturally supposed that Rusty was behind them. He might not be involved at all. A bunch of gunmen, maybe run out of New Mexico, had drifted into south Texas and did what they would do naturally—shoot people. Was that it?

Or *was* Rusty it?

Rusty had done such a good job of scrubbing his character clean that Doreen was ready to get fond of him. Of course, Rusty had a rich father, and Slocum suspected a girl like Doreen would not hold his wealth against him. She might even think of Rusty as a marrying prospect.

He shrugged. His feeling had been that Rusty braced Spotted Jack to step out when Quantrill got mentioned. Quantrill would be the red flag to Spotted Jack, and he'd finish Slocum off.

But would Rusty, just because he'd been chastised in front of the saloon, instigate these attacks? He'd have to be one malevolent hyena for that. Was he? He sounded okay. But something vague floated out from behind his words. Slocum didn't have a handle on it just yet. A feeling, and such feelings in Slocum's experience were never enough. A man could look like a polecat and be a prince, Slocum thought.

He had to withhold judgment on Rusty Hogarth until he got something solid. He should pay a visit to Cassie Gaines and talk to her. Rusty Hogarth was either a yearling who couldn't handle his liquor or he was slick as a weasel.

Meanwhile, Slocum felt he had to keep his gun oiled and stay sharp because, in this town, they were coming at him out of the woodwork, with guns blazing.

He looked at Doreen. She was brushing down her Appaloosa and watching him.

"You certainly were in a study. What on earth were you thinking about?" she asked.

"Wondering who's gonna shoot at me next," he grinned.

She shook her head. "From what I've seen, they're in big trouble if they try. Slocum, you must dine with us. Dad asked to meet you. Can you make it tomorrow for dinner?"

It had been a long time since he had had a good home-cooked meal. "I'll be there, Doreen."

By noon, when Slocum was riding northwest to visit Cassie Gaines, the sun burned hard on the land. She lived out in the range country, soft, lush rolling hills, nourished by small meandering streams. In the distance, because of the clarity of the air, Slocum could see spires of the great mountain stabbing upward, some of them piercing cottony clouds to a halt. It looked like the design of a half-mad sculptor. Below, in the sun, the land looked serene, which, as Slocum well knew, was a thin veil for the struggle for life that went on beneath it.

Then, as if in support of this thought, he saw a hawk dive down in the sky like a falling stone to seize a bird in its claws and heard the cry of death from the victim's throat.

Slocum's instinct was to shoot the hawk, but the damage had been done, and the hawk, if you thought of it, was doing what nature had designed it for, killing to survive.

He stopped at a small stream to refill his canteen, and looked at the colored pebbles in the clear water. A movement along the great rocks caught his eye; it was an antlered deer staring with fear at a crevice, where Slocum suspected lurked a mountain cat in a hunger stalk.

Everything kills to live, most of all man, he thought as he neared the roan. He was startled at the fear in the big eyes, the ears up rigid. Slocum's hand moved to his gun even before he heard the rattle. There it was, near the stone, a foot from his leg, its head back to strike, black beaded eyes, forked tongue swirling. The gun spit fire and part of the rattler's head was suddenly gone. The body curled and writhed. Slocum looked at the roan, still backing off, but the quivering and fear were gone. Curious how the horse could take the roar of his gun calmly but the smell of a rattler could put it into a panic.

As he swung over the saddle, he saw two Comanches on the ridge, staring down. Rifles were slung over their shoulders, and they stood with strong legs apart, like bronze statues. Long-haired, muscled Comanches—they didn't look threatening; seemed content just to observe. He'd fired a shot and they had come out to look. For some reason, they didn't go into hostile action. They may have had something else in mind. Now that they knew he'd fired just to kill a rattler, they disappeared as quickly as they had appeared.

Slocum nudged the roan north. As he rode, his eyes raked the land, the ridges, the rocks, wherever danger might lurk.

* * *

Cassie Gaines lived on land that was smooth, glossy and rich, ran parallel to the river, and stretched out acres and acres. Near the main house was a corral of horses, and as he neared the ranch he could see several cowboys leaning on the fence, watching a rider trying to break a very wild bronco.

Near the corral a woman with gleaming golden hair was fussing over a young colt. It didn't take long for Slocum to be noticed as he rode past the Bar G ranch sign.

The men glanced curiously at him, then back to the bronco. A red-haired cowboy in faded blue jeans kept looking, especially after Cassie started toward him. Then the bronc, a rambunctious critter who had no intention of entertaining a rider, began to heave so viciously that he soon launched the cowboy in an arc through the air and he hit the earth with a thud. He sat up and sputtered curses until the hostile nag started for him, teeth bared, and the cowboy made an undignified run for the fence.

"What other loco wants to try this mangy bone-breaker?" said the cowboy in faded blue jeans.

After a long silence, a lean young cowpoke spoke up. "Lemme at him."

Cassie threw a glance at the young cowboy, shook her head, then came toward Slocum. Her face was grim. "I admire your nerve, coming here, Slocum."

"Got nothing to be feared of, Miss Cassie."

She studied him, her deep brown eyes seeming to glow against her smooth skin and golden hair. He sensed less hostility in her as he tied the roan to the railing.

"What brings you?" she asked.

"Trying to find out who shot your dad, Miss Cassie. That's one way to prove I didn't do it. And I need to ask you a couple of questions."

She glanced away for a moment. "Have you found anything?"

"Just trying. Other than being blamed myself, nobody appears to know too much." His inquiries had produced sketchy theories. Bill Gaines riding west from his ranch met another rider coming east. A fracas apparently developed and he drew his gun but never fired and died with a bullet in his heart.

She bit her lip. "I've heard that you've been attacked yourself by gunfighters. They'd hardly pick on you if you were one of them." She leaned over the fence to watch the men getting the bronc ready for the young cowboy. Slocum, too, leaned on the fence.

"That's mostly what I come about, Miss Cassie. I got hold of Rusty Hogarth and asked if it was true he told you that I did the shooting."

She looked surprised and thought about it. "I'm not sure he named you straight out. Other men said things, too."

"Did he say I shot your dad?"

"I was too excited to make any clear sense of what happened at the time. All I wanted was a name, someone responsible."

"Rusty said he never named me directly."

"I don't think he did, as I remember now. He said a stranger did the shootin'. Then someone came up with your name and I put it together." Her eyes flashed to him. "I realize now it was a mistake. Went off half-cocked. I was practically outa my mind. I'm sorry. Almost got you killed."

Slocum shrugged. So Rusty had told it truthfully after all. He'd been wrong about Rusty. That meant that Slocum would have to start from scratch if he hoped to solve the mystery of who killed Bill Gaines. He wanted to do that. He wanted to help this beautiful woman.

A shout went up from the cowboys as the rider spurred the bronc; it jumped and heaved viciously, throwing the rider through the air, and he thudded to the ground.

Slocum looked critically at the bronc. "One ornery critter."

"His name is Tornado," she said, "and he's unrideable."

"Are you gonna run this ranch by yourself, Miss Cassie?"

"I couldn't handle it. There's a loan out on it, and I just don't know how to make the land pay."

"Looks like a fine piece of land, with riverfront. If you got hold of a good foreman to keep a string on things. Sell horses to the government. Raise cattle, send it to Abilene."

"Sounds easy, but it needs a man's strong hand. I don't have the experience." She looked thoughtful. "Been thinking of selling and joining my aunt in Fort Worth." Then she looked a bit coy. "But everything could change."

"Like what?"

Her eyes met his boldly. "It's personal, Mr. Slocum."

A shout went up as a new rider climbed over Tornado, who took one minute to jolt, jar, and heave him rudely off his back. The horse turned to stare at the downed rider, and Slocum almost laughed at what he

felt was the look of triumph he could almost read in
the horse's features.

"Ornery," he said.

"Unrideable," she said.

"No horse is unrideable," he said.

The rugged cowboy nearby in faded blue denim
turned sharply, and a grim smile twisted his lips.

Cassie looked at him and smiled. "This is John
Slocum. I think you've heard about him. And this is
my honcho, Tim Blake. And Tim thinks, as I can
plainly see, that you might be braggin', Mr. Slocum."

Tim Blake nodded. "He's a bone-buster, that hoss,
Miss Cassie. And no man in his right senses is goin'
to claim he can ride him. Ain't happened yet, and
we've had the best trying, Slocum." He had cool grey
eyes that looked at Slocum without friendliness, as if
he sensed Slocum's interest in Cassie and didn't care
for it.

Slocum leaned on the fence to study the bronc.
There were, as he knew, killer horses that could never
be broken. They'd die first. And this could be one.
He'd seen horses like that, and they sent out a vicious
signal. They made suicidal movements to throw the
rider. Tornado seemed to be like that kind of horse.
The bronc trotted past and his brown eyes went balefully over Slocum, as if he picked up his interest, as
if he knew this two-legged creature was about to yield
to an impulse to dominate him.

The bronc stopped, his eyes on Slocum, as if in
challenge.

It was so odd that the cowboys turned and grinned
at Slocum.

Cassie looked at him, a glint of a smile in her eye.
That did it for him. "Hold the horse," Slocum said.

Two cowhands clambered over the fence and walked toward Tornado, who stood immobile and let them approach.

Before Slocum swung over the saddle he talked gently to the horse, but it was like talking to stone eyes. Underneath him he could feel the back muscles quiver; this animal hated the two-legged creature who tried to dominate him. He stood, frozen, as if the hate inside was building for the explosion. Slocum waited, too, relaxed; he didn't swing his hat or dig his spurs.

The bronc moved slowly, just a calm trot which picked up speed, then it started a suicide rush at the fence. Slocum felt a quiver of tension but held his body balanced. The bronc dug its front legs against the earth in a heart-wrenching stop and heaved, expecting his rider would sail over the fence.

But, to his amazement, the rider stuck. In a fearful rage, Tornado humped and heaved, kicked and leaped with both legs in the air, jerking, twisting, squirming, heaving.

But the hated two-legged creature stayed on. The bronc stood still, quivering, then dashed to the fence and brushed against it, trying to rub the rider off. It didn't work; he stayed on. The bronc, now desperate, crowhopped, lurched, kicked, and heaved, turned with bare teeth to bite at the hated rider. Nothing worked. All he could feel was the gentle but firm pull on his mane. This rider at no time tried to frighten him or strike him.

Suddenly the bronc stopped, his heart pumping in his chest as if it would explode. His rage was gone. He'd done all he could. He had been beat. He stood there quietly, waiting.

As the cowboys cheered, Slocum trotted the horse around the corral, then swung off its back and walked to the fence.

Tim Blake, though he smiled, didn't seem all that pleased. He stood near Cassie as if he had a stake in her, as if he didn't like the idea of anyone but him looking too good in front of her.

Cassie put out her hand, her beautiful face beaming with a broad smile. "Like the way you did that, Slocum. You didn't do it with spurs and a whip. Just wore him down gently. An interesting technique."

Slocum straightened his shirt, which had been twisted by the jolting bronc. He smiled at her. "You don't have to bully a thing to win it."

Cassie tossed her golden hair. "Most cowboys don't believe that, Slocum. What do you think, Tim?"

"A firm hand does a lot of good, Miss Cassie."

Cassie smiled. "See? Can I offer you something before you head back to town, Slocum?"

Tim Blake looked displeased.

"Why, sure. Wouldn't mind some coffee," Slocum said.

"Would you do me a favor, Tim, and ask Rita to bring us coffee and some of her apple pie."

He nodded, looked at Slocum with cool eyes, and turned.

Slocum grinned. "He's in love with you."

They walked toward the side of the house to a long oak table.

She shrugged. "I can't help that, can I?"

"I suppose it'd be easy to fall in love with a woman like you."

Her eyebrows went up. "Are you thinking of it?"

"I think you need a man to help you at this time. All this land."

"I have some ideas," she said.

"What about Tim Blake? Might be a good man for the job."

"He wants it. I'm afraid it's too big a job for him. I just may sell it."

"It's a shame to sell a stretch like this. You've got the river and rich land, fat grass for grazing."

"It's home." She looked disconsolate, and he felt a strong impulse to put his arm around her and give her comfort. She was alone, and it seemed she needed a strong shoulder. Tim Blake cottoned to that idea, but it didn't seem to appeal to her.

"Any time you need my help, Miss Cassie, just gimme a shout."

Her eyes were suddenly melancholy.

"There's one thing I want above all, Slocum. And that's the killer of my father. Help me get him."

His jaw hardened. "I'll do what I can, Miss Cassie."

Slocum had been riding about twenty minutes when he heard the horse behind him. There was no attempt at concealment, so Slocum didn't expect trouble. But in this town, he seemed fair target for just about anyone; he drew his gun and pulled to the side.

Tim Blake came pounding down the trail on a grey gelding. He waved his hand.

"You won't need that," he said, smiling, at the sight of Slocum's gun.

"Never know around these parts."

Blake rode close. He seemed to have things on his mind. "I heard some of the talk back there between you and Miss Cassie about her father."

Slocum's green eyes gleamed. "What do you know about it?"

"Bill Gaines was a straight shooter. Didn't have an enemy in the world. It was a grief to me, to all of us on the ranch, when it happened. We didn't have a notion who did the shootin'. And when your name came up, we were for goin' after you. But that would have been a wrong move, as we found out. We figure it's one of those gunfighters that's drifted into town and are doin' this senseless killin'." He bit his lip. "I hated to hear that Miss Cassie was thinkin' of sellin' out and goin' to Fort Worth. I don't mind tellin' you, I think a lot of the lady." He looked off into the distance. "But I don't think she has any such feelin' for me. Fact is, she tole me so. She's straight as her dad. Still, she could stay here in Dawson. And I heard you say she could lean on me, let me try to run the ranch. That was a mighty nice thing to say, Slocum, and I appreciate it. Trouble is, she's thinkin' more about Rusty Hogarth."

Slocum stared. "Rusty Hogarth! What in hell does she see in a pipsqueak like him?"

"Oh, Rusty is more than he looks. He's been sweet on her for some time. Mr. Hogarth is interested in her land; it runs parallel to his. If they ever put it together, it'd be the richest hunk of territory in southwest Texas."

Slocum studied Tim Blake. He had cool grey eyes in a good-looking face, almost girlishly pretty, and a small mouth. He didn't look hard enough for the challenges of life.

"Something of a prize, a piece of land like hers," Slocum said.

Blake nodded. "Wouldn't surprise me if it wasn't

the land that caught Rusty's attention, aside from the clear fact that Miss Cassie is the most beautiful girl in Dawson."

Slocum grinned. "Natural for all that to grab the eye of a man. You seem to have noticed it."

Blake flushed. "Wouldn't give a damn if she didn't have a dime, Slocum. But she doesn't favor me, and that's the sad truth." He stared off to the horizon. "Fact is, it wouldn't surprise me if she favored *you* a bit."

Slocum smiled gently. "Doubt that I'd stay put for the Garden of Eden." His lips tightened. "But I'd like to help her. Her father was killed. I been blamed, and I been shot at. Don't like any of that. I want to get to the bottom of it. Who killed him? And who is shooting at me, and why?"

Blake nodded. "If you run into anything more than you can handle, call on me." He wheeled the gelding. "Thanks again for your kind words on my behalf."

When Slocum rode into Main Street, he saw some cowboys lolling on the boardwalk, a couple of old-timers on the porch in front of the saloon, and some shoppers gathered near Cutter's General Store.

Slocum lifted himself off the saddle and let the roan drink at a water trough. He leaned against a wooden post, pulled a havana from his pocket, and had just lit it when he saw the buggy come down the street.

Luke Hogarth was driving, snapping the whip, talking earnestly to Lulabelle. Behind the buggy, Rusty rode on a pinto, followed by three husky cowboys.

When Luke saw Slocum he smiled graciously and called out, "Come see me soon, Mr. Slocum." Slocum tipped his hat. Lulabelle stared at him, pretty and insolent, with no change of expression. *Tough little filly,* Slocum thought. Rusty stared at him, his face cold, and the cowboys behind stared at Slocum as they rode past with flat, curious eyes.

Slocum watched them sweep out of town, as did the other spectators. The Hogarths. They were a power in town all right. And the more he saw of the father, the more he wondered how he had spawned such children.

5

The dance that night was spirited, a lot of fun and jollity. The boys were all spruced up, the girls prettied up, the punch spiked up, and everyone was merry.

When he danced with Doreen, she whispered, "We're making a feast for you tomorrow. Don't let anything keep you from coming."

"I'm drooling already, Miss Doreen," he said, but he was thinking of more than her dinner.

The cowboys danced and stomped, and when they got thirsty, they went out back of the barn to guzzle from pint bottles. Though the dance was noisy, surprisingly no cowboy went off half-cocked. The ladies seemed to be a gentling influence.

Though Cassie Gaines came, she didn't seem to be dancing. Perhaps she needed the mood of a party, or perhaps she'd come hoping to get a lead on the gunman she wanted. Tim Blake stayed close to her, and to Slocum it was clear that he was hopelessly in love.

To Slocum's displeasure, as well as to Blake's, the only time Cassie did dance was with Rusty Hogarth. During the dance he talked earnestly to her, and he made her smile twice. Slocum glanced at Blake. His grey eyes burned with jealousy. Nothing good will come of this, Slocum thought as he drifted to the punch bowl. Standing there, sipping from his glass, he noticed Lulabelle Hogarth dancing with a husky blond cowboy. She was a standout in her silken low-cut dress that partly revealed a hefty breast. Slocum couldn't help but remember what she looked like naked. As if she caught his thought, she glanced at him, and their eyes locked. He couldn't tell if she was reading his mind, but her gaze, as usual, was insolent. One high-falutin filly, and he couldn't help thinking it would be nice to spank her bare bottom and bring her down a peg.

Just then, Cassie Gaines came up to the punch bowl and nodded at him, her eyes mocking.

"You looked at Lulabelle like a coyote at a rabbit," she said.

"Looks more like a wildcat than a rabbit to me," he said.

Cassie dipped into the bowl with her glass. "Well, it's been said she has claws."

"All the better to tear you with, I'm sure."

"I think you're hard on her. But then, you're probably interested. All men are."

"I don't know her, but she makes me think of the widow spider who eats her lovers."

Cassie laughed. "S'posed to be rough on men, but I always found her nice."

He turned to her. "None of my business, of course, but what do you see in a man like Rusty Hogarth? Figured you for more taste. And Tim Blake's the better man."

Her brown eyes glinted dangerously. "You're right. It's none of your business, Mr. Slocum."

"I say what I think, Miss Cassie. Sorry if I offended you. Like to dance?"

"I'm not in the mood for dancing." Her golden hair glittered in the light, and her beautiful face looked at him seriously, then her lips formed a curious smile. "It so happens, Slocum, that you look like the best of them all. But I'm not angling for you. There's more to a man than the speed of his draw or the size of his fist. I'm interested in a man's mind, in his vision of the future of this territory. I think Rusty Hogarth has a mind like that." Her mouth was tight. "What are *you* building, Mr. Slocum?"

She was angry and she looked beautiful. "I'm just trying to stay alive," he drawled. "Don't know if I'll see tomorrow, the way folks are throwing bullets at me." He sipped from his glass and felt a spasm of irritation at her attack. "Far as I'm concerned, you can hitch up with a mule, Miss Cassie."

Her lovely mouth twisted. "If I was thinking of a mule, I might consider you, Mr. Slocum."

He gritted his teeth and looked at the dancers. Just then Rusty Hogarth came toward them with a slight swagger and a sardonic grin on his youthful face.

He spoke to Slocum. "Isn't she the most beautiful girl in South Texas, mister?"

Slocum, whose thought was *Much too good for you,* watched him gallantly turn and bow. "May I beg the pleasure of another dance, Miss Cassie? Such a pity to waste this good music."

She gazed at him quizzically, then smiled. "Be glad to dance, Rusty."

They went off into the whirl of the dancing, and as Slocum watched he heard Blake behind him. "See, she's got a soft spot for him. A polecat like him."

Slocum shrugged philosophically. "Women don't understand men. I've seen them go crazy in love over the mangiest of men." He turned up his palms. "It's a mystery. Women are a mystery."

They watched the dancers in silence for a time, then Slocum said, "When it comes down to it, there's nothing we can hang on Rusty. He may not be our kind of man, but she likes what he's got. He's got vision, she says."

"Vision," Blake snorted. "Yeah, he's got that. He sees clear as hell her fat piece of land. I can tell a man by his smell, Slocum. And Rusty Hogarth stinks."

Slocum shrugged: male jealousy, and that was that.

Then he noticed Doreen dancing past, her partner a cowboy in a brightly spangled shirt.

"There's a nice girl for you, Blake."

But Blake couldn't take his eyes off Cassie, and as he watched the dance, his eyes grew somber.

Later in the evening, Rusty came alongside Slocum, and with a boyish grin asked, "Did you get yourself straight, Slocum? Those questions that bothered you? Did you talk to Cassie?"

Slocum nodded. "She tells it the way you did."

Rusty showed his palms, as if he had nothing to

hide. "That's how it was."

Slocum's eyes narrowed. "Something else bothers me, Rusty, and I been meaning to bring it up."

Rusty looked at him, clear-eyed and smiling, a man with a clear conscience.

"How do you explain Burt and Jed, a couple of mangy gunmen, accusing me of the Gaines killing? Saying it was *you* they heard it from."

Rusty stared disbelievingly, then grinned. "That's it. It was the same thing. We were all together, talkin' about it —who done the killin'. Because I was there, and because the Hogarths count for somethin' in this town, they did the same thing Cassie did. They imagined it was me who said you shot Gaines. I said, 'It was a stranger,' that's all. Then your name came up, as a new man in town. People just went off half-cocked." Again he held out his palms.

Slocum's grim face cracked a little. "If I ever need a slick-talking lawyer in court, Rusty, I hope you let me call on you."

Rusty glared, annoyed. Then he smiled. "You're funnin', of course. I s'pose it's a compliment. But here we are talkin' when we should be dancin'. Ever see so many pretty fillies, Slocum?"

It was true, Slocum thought; the town had them.

They stood there watching the dancers. Then, to Slocum's surprise, he saw Cassie dancing by with Tim Blake. The glow in Blake's eyes was clear enough, and Rusty didn't miss it. He watched, his lips pressed tight. Cassie looked at him across the floor. "That's my beauty," Rusty said.

Slocum turned to him. "You seem mighty interested in her."

Rusty nodded, his eyes cold. "Mighty interested. I aim to marry her."

Several times during the evening, Slocum found himself looking at Lulabelle Hogarth. She was the kind of woman that men looked at. Several came to her asking her to dance, but she would smile and decline. She danced only with the blond man, rough-cut, with a jaw like iron. Someone called him Hardy. He was a vigorous man with bulky shoulders, a slugger, the kind who would probably appeal to her. She saw Slocum looking at her and, again, instead of turning away, stared brashly. Hardy, noticing her stare, looked at Slocum coldly.

Slocum reached into his pocket for a havana and lit it. Again her nakedness, as he remembered it, came to his mind. *She sure has hit me hard,* he thought. A devilish urge to ask her for a dance came to him, and he almost laughed aloud at its idiocy. She would probably sprout those claws and tear him to pieces.

When the dance broke up, people milled around as if hating to go home, though some did go to their buggies and horses. Doreen, he noted, had gone off with the silver-spangled cowboy. Cassie was standing with Rusty and Tim Blake far behind the barn, where the Gaines buggy was tied.

A big silver moon hung in the great dark sky, and Slocum admired it as he smoked. He heard the swish of a dress and smelled the fragrant smell of a woman.

Lulabelle and Hardy were passing in front of him. He couldn't help looking at the flesh of her breasts that pushed against her dress.

She stopped, and her dark brown eyes glowed. "You're Slocum, aren't you?"

He nodded.

She turned to Hardy, who was looking at him without enthusiasm. "This is Slocum. He likes to watch ladies at their bath, Hardy."

Slocum was thunderstruck; he knew she was one rough filly but he scarcely expected anything like that. And if Hardy was the man he looked like, all hell would shortly break loose.

Hardy gaped at her. "Did I hear you correct, Lulabelle?"

"You heard me, honey," she said, smiling, aware that she had thrown a spark in oily waters.

Hardy stepped forward, thrusting his iron jaw at Slocum. "Do I understand, mister, that you were spying on Lulabelle while she was bathing?"

The moment was so tense that Slocum felt like laughing. He had watched Lulabelle, but he'd come on her by accident. And she had seemed to find as much pleasure in displaying herself as he had in looking. She was something of a bitch who liked the excitement of men in combat over her. She'd done it deliberately.

"Don't get excited, Hardy. I was riding along the trail and the lady was bathing. Nothing I could do but look at her. Would you turn away, Hardy?"

He had deep brown eyes and they blazed. "Well, you're one nervy son of a bitch." He peeled his jacket and waved a big fist with thick, muscular fingers. "Gonna teach you to respect a woman."

Slocum shook his head; was there no way to avoid a fight or a showdown in Dawson?

"Listen, Hardy. I'm just a bit weary of fighting in this town. And, just between you and me, what I saw ain't worth the bruises we're going to put on each other."

Hardy stared in amazement. "If you ain't the mangiest dog I ever met!" He rolled up his shirt to show an enormous bicep. "Pardon me, Lulabelle, while I massacre a low-down peepin' polecat."

Slocum sighed deeply; no matter what he did, he couldn't avoid a fight in Dawson. He pulled off his gunbelt and squared away. Hardy looked like his name, hard as a rock, with an iron jaw. He looked like a battler, too, his broad face decorated with the cuts and scars of fights. His nose came out strongly from his face and looked like a fine target. Hardy put up his two fists in front of him and moved on Slocum. Did he know the art of fighting or was he just a brawler, Slocum wondered?

Hardy, fists clenched hard, threw a haymaker, then a wild left. Slocum laughed. He was a bruiser with no art, but with a knockout punch if he caught you right. Slocum jabbed quickly with his left at Hardy's nose. A solid thump. Hardy looked astonished. He didn't like his nose to be hit. He rushed, swung rights and lefts which Slocum blocked and countered with a hard right again on Hardy's nose. Hardy grunted as his nose spouted blood.

Hardy roared and rushed forward, grabbed Slocum around the waist, and squeezed. Slocum brought the heel of his palm up sharply under Hardy's bleeding nose.

Hardy yelped with pain and put his hand to his nose. The sight of the blood put him into a fearful rage, and he rushed in as Slocum drove a hard right to his nose.

Hardy stopped, petrified and insulted. "You son of a bitch," he roared, "why don't you fight like a man?" Slocum punctuated the remark with a left to the nose. By this time Hardy's nose was swollen, misshapen, puffy, and bleeding.

And Hardy was fit to be tied. He put up his right to guard his face, and Slocum threw a pounding right at his gut. He doubled over, cursing, then rushed, throwing his great hamlike fists wildly, missing, trying to grab his opponent. Slocum danced this way and that, opening Hardy's guard until he threw a sledge-hammer punch at Hardy's jaw.

Hardy went down and stayed there.

Slocum shook his head. "Fighting's not your game, Hardy." He looked at Lulabelle. Her breasts were heaving, her eyes gleaming, and she was staring at him. He couldn't tell whether she wanted to eat him alive or grab his body.

A wild filly, he thought. He strapped on his gunbelt and looked around. Cowboys were grinning from ear to ear; a bully had been put to rest.

From the other side of the barn came the sound of shrill voices, then a gunshot. Slocum followed the crowd.

Tim Blake was lying on the ground, his gun in hand, unfired, blood streaming from his chest. Standing nearby was Rusty Hogarth.

Slocum pushed forward and bent to Blake; he was a goner. Hard-eyed, he looked at Rusty.

"He called me a name," Rusty said, and turned to the two bulky men who always seemed to be near him. "You heard him."

Blake twisted a bit, his mouth working, and Slocum bent to hear him whisper. He couldn't make out the words. He put his ear to the lips.

"Don't let the bastard get her, Slocum," Blake whispered. His eyes looked fearful and they froze with that look.

The sky was streaked with bits of crimson fire as Slocum rode the roan on the trail to Doreen's place. She lived out near White Bird Creek, an isolated area near a great gathering of rocky land. As he rode, he stayed aware of the land, of the lone buzzard circling lazily in the sky, waiting with inborn patience for the animal below to die. He was aware of the pink and violet flowers that dotted the edge of the creek, of the piney scent that came on the lift of the breeze. He pleasured in the sounds of nature, even the creak of the saddle leather, as he rode. The land seemed to be flowering; nature was in harmony.

All is peaceful but man, Slocum told himself once again.

He thought of Tim Blake, dead because, in a moment of jealousy, he'd said the wrong thing to Rusty. With his last breath, he'd whispered, "Don't let the bastard get her." He hated Rusty. Poor Tim thought he might cure Cassie of her interest in Rusty by shooting. Blake just didn't know his limitations; he wasn't good enough with a gun to challenge Rusty.

And he hadn't done much good by dying.

A senseless fight. Or was it? Not for Rusty, perhaps. With Tim Blake out of the way, Cassie Gaines had lost the one man who might run her ranch. It made her more beholden to Rusty. And, according to Blake, Rusty found the beautiful land and the beautiful

Cassie an irresistible combination.

Slocum shook his head; good fortune sometimes even came to a polecat. But why, he wondered, did he think of Rusty as a polecat when he had no proof? Everything Rusty had claimed seemed to be true. If it hadn't been for that ugly run-in at the saloon, Slocum could have no reason to believe Rusty a polecat. Well, he just wasn't Slocum's kind of man.

Then he thought of Lulabelle. A fascinating lady, that one. Why did she turn Hardy loose on him? Ornery, that's why. Made a big deal about that bathing. If she really was modest, she'd never have come out of that stream when he was standing there. A woman who got her kicks watching men fight over her. A bad filly. Slocum sighed; a woman like her might be the devil's own pleasure. He felt horny as hell.

Up ahead, near thick low brush, he saw a movement. His gun was out in a flash, but he held his fire as he sighted Doreen Smith. She was smiling. She'd come out to head him off, and he couldn't help looking with pleasure at her. She wore a fresh pink shirt and a blue calico skirt. She looked cute as a ladybug, and her smile was enticing. He swung off the roan and came toward her.

"Thought I'd come up and meet you, just so you don't get lost." Her smile was wicked.

"Couldn't get lost if I was near you, Doreen."

She looked like peaches and cream; she had a pretty kissing mouth with a ripe underlip, and a rounded bosom which pushed against her tight dress.

She laughed. "You know how to make a girl feel wanted, Slocum."

They walked side by side. "Once you meet Dad,

I won't get a word in edgewise," she said. "Thought I'd pick you up a bit early. Maria hasn't quite made the fixin's."

His pulse quickened. Was she planning a game? If so, it couldn't come at a better time.

They were, he noticed, in the dense part of the brush, a most discreet place.

"If we have some extra time, maybe we could put it to good use, Doreen."

"That would be nice, Slocum." Bold as brass, she put up her pretty mouth. He pulled her close, planted his mouth on hers.

The flesh in his breeches jumped. She felt it, and gave a small sigh of pleasure. His hands moved to her shapely buttocks and he pulled her tight against him as he kissed her again. Her mouth was fresh as peppermint. He pulled her into the thicket, slipped his hand under her skirt, felt the silk of her leg, and slipped his hand past the chemise between her thighs. She was warm and wet. He stroked her for a time, touching the pleasure nerve. It made her inhale sharply. He opened his britches and her hand took his proud flesh and stroked it.

"Let's get these duds off," he whispered.

They peeled and he looked at her.

He delighted in the delicate beauty of her body, the slender girlish waist, the almost womanly hips, the finely shaped thighs and the lovely pink lips that pouted at him with such sexy impudence. He felt a powerful impulse and brought his face between her thighs. She leaned back and groaned as he pleasured in her body. Then he twisted his own body, offering her his rigid maleness. Driven by instinct, she put her lips against it, kissing it, bringing her tongue to it, then the warmth of her mouth. He watched her for a time, then felt the climbing rush of tension. He threw his body over hers and, as her thighs spread, he pierced her.

She whimpered as he thrust, and grabbed his body. They stayed tight, then he caressed her—her buttocks, her breasts, the small curve of her back. He began to move, pulling out and slipping in, holding hard to her buttocks.

He built a strong, powerful rhythm which she picked up. Then her body tightened and she thrust against him as if she felt intense pain. She did it again, groaning, and, after a few moments, gave another convulsive shudder. His own movements never stopped as he felt dynamite build up in his body, and for excruciating moments he soared, then exploded. She moaned, and frantically thrust against him.

They lay together quietly while he thought that, young as she was, she had to be the nicest piece of pastry in South Texas.

She combed her hair and fixed herself so that before they started for her home she would look proper and prim.

6

Doreen Smith lived in a comfortable house on a fair-sized piece of land. There were chickens prowling the pen, a buggy in the stable, and a corral with two horses.

Her father, a rugged, strong-faced man with iron-grey hair, looked as if he'd spent his time trying to beat down the ornery problems of frontier life.

"So you're Slocum." He shook hands heartily. "Wanta thank you for helpin' Doreen t'other day. She tole me what happened out there front of Bryan's Saloon."

"Glad to be helpful, Mr. Smith."

"Amos is the name, Slocum. And I'm proud to shake your hand." They sat around a table near the corral that gave a good view of the land. Amos poured whiskey into the glasses and held one out to Slocum.

He had penetrating grey eyes and a powerful neck and shoulders. Before he lifted his drink, he turned to Doreen, who'd been watching him with a smile.

"Maria can use your help makin' dinner, Doreen."

She grinned. "All right, Dad. Jest don't drink up all the whiskey. Don't want you too drunk to enjoy Maria's special cookin' tonight."

Amos smiled, watching her leave. "She's a honey. She's the reason I come out here, trying to start a new life. We're from Oklahoma. Lost her mother comin' across the land. Indians." His eyes went sombre for a moment, then he raised his glass. "Let's drink up."

The liquor went down smooth, and Slocum smiled as Amos quickly refilled both glasses. Clearly a drinking man.

"Heard about you, Slocum." Amos smoothed his chin. "You seem to be the only man with the guts to save this town."

Slocum looked at his glass. The liquor had hit Amos in the head mighty fast. He himself didn't feel it. He gazed at the land. It rolled, climbed gently, the grass looked rich, and far off the sun bulked like a big orange over the purple mountains. Just a mile away, the land went rocky and steep.

"A clean, beautiful land, Amos," Slocum said, feeling a touch of reverence toward so much beauty.

"Yeah, it's beautiful. And it's land that's been bought dearly, with blood. " His grey eyes fixed on Slocum. "Some of the finest men I've known have gone down in the battle over it." His eyes misted. "We fought, we been fightin' as long as I can remember. We fought the bluecoats, fought the Comanches. And when you think you got a nice something you can hang on to, somewhere to plant your roots, what do you s'pose happens?"

Slocum's green eyes gleamed. He liked this man, a sturdy frontier man, the kind that helped make the territory.

"What happens, Amos?" he said softly.

"The spoilers come in. They always come in when the fightin's over and pickin's are right."

"What do you mean—the spoilers?"

"There's a bunch of outlaws driftin' in and outa this town, Slocum. They're feedin' off it like vultures. Don't know what they want, but they're breakin' down the life of this town. I've seen this thing happen before. A good place gets torn apart. Maybe it's always happened in history, Slocum. Where there's a feast, the vultures come in."

Slocum listened grimly, sipping his glass, watching the grey eyes across the table smolder with anger.

"This is a town where you don't know, day to day, if you're gonna live or die, Slocum. I haven't been here that long, but I got to know a few ranchers. Some are already dead. Gaines, Sam Walker, Archie Brown, Lem Comstock."

He poured another drink and brought the glass to his lips. "I tole some of the ranchers we should get together and do some shootin' of our own. But I couldn't get them to ride. They say these men are gunfighters, and they're afraid."

When Slocum finished his glass, Amos didn't waste a moment to refill it.

"Yes, I heard about you, Slocum. Everyone has. You just happened to drift into town, mebbe on your way somewhere. But lightning started to flash 'round your head. Some of the gunfighters singled you out and have come to grief. Heard about Jed and Burt who tried to take you on at one time." Amos whistled with appreciation. "Two mangy gunmen cut down at once."

"What I'd a given to see that." He raised his glass as if in a toast. "Can't tell you how much I admire that. You don't live in this town, mister, but what you're doin' may be savin' its life." He drank and wiped his mouth. "Just keep on mowin' them down, and we might have a peaceful town again. Mebbe they'll jest go away. The danger is that *you* might go away before the job is done." He stood up, his eyes shining. "I talked to some of the men, and we'd like to make you a handsome offer of money and land to stay and help us. How 'bout it?"

Slocum smiled. "Tell you the truth, Amos, all I been doing is defending myself. I'm not a peace officer and don't aim to be one. I got blamed for the killing of Bill Gaines. I didn't even know the gent. Miss Cassie Gaines heard, wrongly, that it was me. I didn't like that a bit. And I stayed in Dawson just to see if I could find out who did the killing. When I find that out, I hope to do something about it. Then I'll probably be moseying on."

Amos squinted at him. "So you're helpin' Miss Cassie. That's fine. Find the killer, and take proper care o' him. Charlie Higgins has seen you draw. Says it's the fastest gun he's ever seen. If you stick around long enough, you could just clean up things here by your single solitary self."

Slocum shrugged. "I'm not looking to kill any man, Amos. I'm sure Higgins is exaggerating. There's always a man out there just a hair's-breadth faster, and honestly, I don't care to meet him. I just intend to go about my business. If someone steps in front of me, why then I'll just have to defend myself. That's nature's law—the law of survival."

It was then that Doreen came out and said, "Dinner's ready—and you better come quick. Maria and me didn't break our necks to let this dinner get cold."

A marvelous whiff of roast chicken and gravy and all the fixings came out to Slocum. "Smells like good Georgia eatin', Doreen." His eyes strayed to the beautiful lines of her body, and he grinned.

He left the Smith homestead when the moon was low in the sky, a big yellow moon that threw a flood of light on the earth. It brightened the trunks of the trees and cast deep shadows off the rocks.

Slocum rode slowly, with a fine feeling of content after a feast of roast chicken, yams, the fixings, and apple pie. His body, too, felt content. He grinned at the thought of Doreen; she might be a young filly, but when it came to womanly wiles she was old as time. He surely had pleasured in her.

As he rode he thought of what Amos had said about the gunmen drifting into Dawson. They were there all right. Where had they come from? he wondered. They had Robber Roosts in New Mexico where outlaws gathered, safe from pursuit of the law. It was mighty dangerous for lawmen to ride into such outlaw territory. Still, every so often, a vigilante bunch might gather to raid the Robber Roost. The outlaws would make a run. They just moved on. Well, they could have just moved, some of them, to a hideaway near

Dawson where, because they were gunmen, they practiced their craft. Several ranchers had already bit the dust. The killings seemed to be random. An outlaw, feeling drunk or mean, would chance on someone. There'd be a spark, a showdown, then a killing. That was how it often happened in this territory, where the only law was the gun.

He himself had been slugged and shot at ever since he hit Dawson. It was a mean town. Yet, according to the townsfolk, it had been peaceful until lately. Until just before he hit the town, one could say.

Slocum thought of the dead men named by Hawkins. Why these men? Were they just unlucky enough to stumble into quarrelsome gunmen?

Slocum, whose eyes always moved restlessly on the trail, suddenly felt a tingle and pulled sharply on the roan. He'd seen something on the ground. He always looked there because that was where the history of what happened before he got there was written. Clear as words in a book, if you knew how to read it.

The prints of two unshod ponies came out of a thicket. Comanches. Fresh prints, within the hour. Headed northwest, toward the place where he'd come from. There was only one homestead there.

Slocum's piercing green eyes searched the land. He felt uneasy. He had seen two Comanches earlier and, at the time, felt they were not hostile. But if horses, women, and whiskey came into the picture, they could turn hostile.

His skin prickled. The Smith homestead was isolated and unfortified.

He might be jumping at shadows. Maybe not. Two Comanche braves on an expedition of mayhem? He'd seen it happen plenty of times. He might be mistaken, but he had to warn Amos Smith, just so he wouldn't be a sitting duck.

He followed the prints, his eyes sharp, his ears listening for any movement caused by human presence. The sudden fluttering of a bird, the circling of a flock over food in a camp, the unnatural movement of a leaf—anything that sent the signal of deadly ambush.

Though the prints moved in a devious pattern, the direction went steadily northwest.

The bright moon made tracking easier. Slocum's one hope, as he moved nearer the Smith place, was that the Comanches would not attack, it being night. Comanches feared that death at night left the spirits to wander restlessly. But some Comanches still did attack at night.

When he saw that the prints turned, it sent a chill to his spine. They were headed for the Smith homestead, beyond a doubt. Two prowling braves, thirsty for liquor, hungry for revenge, hungry for a woman.

The prints went through a passage through rocks, through dense brush, then edged to the Smith homestead,

He swung off the roan, picketed it to a branch, and went forward in a crouch. The house looked peaceful enough in the cool, silver light of the moon, but it wasn't. Something was wrong. The corral was empty, a door to the house was open. He moved quietly.

The horses were gone, so chances were the Comanches would be, too. He hoped the horses would satisfy the Comanches, but that open door was worrisome.

His gun out, he came into the house. He found

Maria first, a heavy woman, her eyes wide in terror, bruises on her throat. She'd been grabbed from behind, her cry smothered. Amos lay on the floor of the living room, a bloodstain on his chest, an unfired pistol in his hand.

With dread, Slocum looked into the last room. Empty. Had Doreen escaped? He examined the floor. Scuffling; they had taken her.

That was a crucial mistake, he thought. She would slow them down; it left them vulnerable—that is, unless they did quickly what they wanted...

With his hunting instincts fiercely alive, he remounted the roan and followed the prints as they climbed the ridge, moving to a trail between a pile-up of rocks. The Comanches had taken the girl, two horses, and four bottles of whiskey, and they were climbing into rock country, where they could bunk for the night safely.

As Slocum moved, he thought about it. They would drink the whiskey, then amuse themselves with Doreen. After that, anything could happen.

Minutes could mean her life.

He pushed the roan up the twisting trail, his gun in hand, his eyes raking the rocks, the crevices, the nooks.

Now the moon was high, a full, silver disk, its light shining brightly. But if he could track, they, too, could see, if they were looking. They would hardly believe someone had already discovered their dirty work. A nighttime hush hung over the land. Even the sound of a night animal would be disturbingly loud.

The Comanches, Slocum decided, would not be far from this point. Though they had struck at night,

Comanches hated to travel at night. They would probably start at the crack of dawn, but just now they were in some cozy nook, either drinking or sleeping.

He gritted his teeth; the thought of Doreen at their mercy made his veins swell. Yes, they'd be drinking and would feel damned safe, thinking nobody would discover their crime before daybreak. He had an edge.

He moved silently, step by step, never putting his foot down where it might make a sound. He was tracking the Comanche, and nobody could read the signs and sounds of nature better than an Indian.

He remembered these Comanches, what they looked like, powerful and dangerous. The young Comanche brave always thirsted for vengeance. This had been his land, and he hated the palefaces who had grabbed it, who had tried to destroy his people.

Slocum's jaw hardened; the struggle between the red and white man was unending, a deadly fight that could only finish one way. But, before his inevitable defeat, the Comanche would spare none in his bloody revenge.

Slocum crept higher, his gun ready. He couldn't afford to lose concentration, not for a moment. He had forgotten about Cassie Gaines, the mystery death of her father, the gunmen in Dawson, the riddle of Rusty. All wiped out in his focus on what lay in front.

The Comanches could strike from anywhere, silent and deadly as the cobra. He had one hope: the Comanches' deep thirst for whiskey. They drank to get drunk. They'd taken four bottles of whiskey, and Slocum had reason to believe they would guzzle plenty.

Even now they might be in a drunken snooze up among the jutting rocks, piled to a height of about thirty feet. What about Doreen? He hated to think of her.

He inched forward, following the prints until he came to a twist in the trail.

He listened. For what? This looked like secure cover. He would himself pick such a spot to sack in for the night.

He could hear breathing. It was his own. He held his breath, fearful that the Comanches would pick it up.

Then he heard it, the sound, scarcely a sound, the whisper of breechclout against stone, and his instincts worked quicker than his mind. He fired at the top of the smooth, high rock from where a fierce-faced Comanche was looking down, his rifle raised to shoot. A blaze of red blossomed in the Comanche's forehead as he pitched back.

Slocum flung himself to the ground, again instinctively, and rolled as two bullets struck the place he'd been. As he rolled Slocum fired at the other side of the rock where another fierce blunt face glared down. The bullet sheared a piece of skull and went flying as the Comanche, in death, fired a third bullet by reflex; then his body fell to the rocks below with a sickening thud.

Two dead. Slocum became aware of sticky sweat on his body. He moved slowly, because you never knew what still might be lurking. But there was nothing, just the broken bodies of two Comanches.

He found Doreen back in the rocks, tied hand and foot, a piece of her dress stuffed in her mouth to keep her silent. The horses were tied still farther back. The whiskey bottles were empty, two of them smashed against the rocks.

They had been enjoying the whiskey too much to enjoy Doreen, it turned out. They had just begun to think of her when one of the Comanches heard Slocum, and they set up the ambush.

He untied her and she flung her arms around him, her eyes hollow with despair. She knew what had happened back in her house.

For a long time she trembled in his arms before they started back.

7

Slocum sat at the bar, whiskey in front of him, looking in the mirror behind the bar at the reflection of four men playing poker. They were a grim-looking lot, scraggy-bearded, with soiled shirts and jeans, but they talked in low voices and played quietly.

Slocum had come to the saloon for a couple of whiskeys to ease the pain of memory and to do a bit of thinking.

He hated what had happened yesterday at the Amos Smith homestead, Doreen made an orphan suddenly by the violence in the territory. She couldn't stay there by herself, and even now was on the stagecoach to join her uncle at San Antonio.

She was, after all, a young filly, though in this territory you didn't stay young for long, and what had happened had left her in shock. She'd been lucky to escape ravishment by the Comanches, but the sudden brutal death of her father and Maria had left its mark.

When word got around, neighbors came to pay their respects. Among them was Luke Hogarth who had known her father. He looked genuinely grieved by what had happened. Slocum, standing near Doreen, heard Hogarth speak.

"Miss Doreen, I can't tell you how much I grieve for what happened. I knew your father. He was among the last of the red-blooded men who helped carve out the Texas territory. It puts me in a fearful rage that his life was ended like that. It proves that none of us can be safe until every Comanche is either stamped out or roped off on a reservation." He paused. "I thank heaven that a man like John Slocum happened to be near enough to protect you. Our daughters and our wives are not safe as long as one Comanche rides this territory."

He patted her hand. "I been told you wish to join your kin in San Antonio, and that you're short of ready cash. It'd be a pleasure for me to help you. You might be thinkin' of sellin' your land. I tell you frankly, I don't need it. Got more land than I need. But that don't stop me from making you a fine offer of three hundred dollars. Most likely, that could help you start again. What do you say?"

Doreen, overcome by this generous offer, flung her arms around him and burst into tears.

Slocum couldn't help being impressed, though he wished Hogarth didn't have to point out how big-hearted he was being, buying land he didn't need.

The price was indeed generous for such land, and Slocum had to admire Luke Hogarth. Clearly his reputation for being a four-square, straight, high-minded man had not been exaggerated.

Slocum's thoughts were jarred by a loud voice from one of the players at the card table, and he looked up at them in the mirror. A bearded, surly man in a soiled green shirt had cursed at the dealer for giving him rotten cards.

"Damn you, Hawk, you're givin' me the worst damn cards in the deck."

The dealer, a lean-faced man with cold grey eyes, stared grimly at him.

"I ain't givin' 'em to you, you idiot. Them's how the cards arc stacked."

"Are you shore it's not *you* that's stackin' 'em, Hawk?"

Hawk glared. "If I didn't know you were funnin' you'd have a bullet in your gut, Gordy."

Gordy glared back. "Maybe the bullet'd be in your gut."

Slocum, aware that sudden mayhem could erupt wherever men drank and gambled, studied the situation. If they drew, he could, at his location, end up with a wandering bullet. These men looked a hard-bitten lot. They could even fit the description he'd heard of the drifting gunmen.

Then a third player, big and brawny, spoke to establish the peace. "Will you two locos shut up and play poker? I got a decent hand for a change." He grinned. "If you're gonna fight, pick a draw when my hand is bad."

The humor seemed to break the ice, and the two men, after exchanging dirty looks, resumed play.

The saloon doors swung open. Higgins stood there, looked around, then took a spot next to Slocum.

"Nice to see you."

Slocum nodded.

The barman brought a bottle and a glass to Higgins.

"Shame about Amos Smith," Higgins said, his face grim.

Slocum lifted his glass.

Higgins drank off his shot and wiped his mouth. "Amos knew what's been happening in this town," he said in a low voice.

Slocum nodded. "He said, 'Where there's a feast, the vultures come in.'"

Higgins poked a thumb at the men playing cards. "The vultures."

Slocum gazed at them in the mirror. "Seem to be mindin' their own business."

"No one here that interests them. That can be the only reason."

Slocum frowned. "Do you think they're shootin' at special people?"

"That thought did cross my mind."

"Why?"

"Dunno why. If I did, it all might make sense."

Slocum shook his head. "Looks like nothing to me. A gunfighter gets mean with drinking, bumps into a rancher, there's insults, then shootings. Looks like nothing more than that."

"Looks like that," Higgins had to admit. "Still, it has a smell."

They were silent and each lifted his glass.

Then Higgins said, "I hear Doreen Smith has left town."

Slocum nodded. "Luke Hogarth did a nice thing,

gave her three hundred dollars for land that wasn't worth one hundred."

Higgins's light blue eyes gazed at Slocum. "Did the same to the widow of Lem Comstock and Sam Walker. Gave the ladies three hundred apiece. Not worth that kind of money. And Hogarth doesn't need the land. He's land rich. Just a kind-hearted man."

Slocum nodded. It was decent. Or was it good business? Luke Hogarth probably combined a good heart with a good business head. He might be taking a long view of the territory. Maybe he had a vision that someday all this land might come to flower. Not in his time, but in some future. So he might be investing for his heirs. Though, in Slocum's view, his heirs, Rusty and Lulabelle, looked like they deserved nothing but an acre of cactus. Just spoiled brats. Sometimes it happened that good stock went bad in the offshoots. But maybe he misjudged Rusty. Cassie Gaines seemed to be sweet on him. He had vision, she had said, "of what this country will be like."

Slocum bit his lip in vexation. And Cassie had been critical of him. "What are you building, Mr. Slocum?" *Building!* He had his hands full trying to stay alive in this town where the air was thick with bullets. This was not a time for building but for surviving.

There was a growl at the card table, and a sputter of curses. Slocum swung around. The sounds were ominous.

Hawk pushed away from the table. "I tole you, Gordy, to stop cussing me for your stinkin' cards."

"Every time you deal, I get stinkin' cards. Why is that, Hawk?"

"'Cause you're a stinkin' hyena, I reckon."

Gordy pushed back his chair, his eyes burning.

"Them's your last livin' words, you low-down polecat."

Everyone scrambled for the sides of the saloon.

Slocum, realizing that he stood directly behind Hawk, hit the floor just a moment before the bullet flew, burying itself in the bar wood just where he'd been standing.

Both men had missed.

Then Curly yelled and stepped between them. "Hold it, you goddamn fools. What are you fightin' about? Nothin'. Just because you got a crawful of whiskey. Now put up your guns."

Both men, sullen-faced, stared at each other, as if whatever they wanted, it hadn't happened yet. They holstered their guns.

"That's it," Curly said, grinning, turning to stare at the men in the bar, sneaking a glance at Slocum who, he realized, had been in the line of fire. "Now everything's fine. No more playing today. We're leavin'."

Slocum got slowly to his feet and turned to look at the bullet in the wood. If he had not hit the floor, it would have gutted him. It had been fired by Gordy, who faced him. He was the last of the four men who had started for the door. Slocum looked at him, at his surly glowering face, his grey, deep-pitted eyes, his hard-bitten mouth.

He glanced suddenly at Slocum, and an evil grin twisted his features, which suddenly spoke volumes to Slocum.

"Just a minute, Gordy," he said quietly, and putting the muscle pack of his shoulder behind it, he swung at Gordy's jaw. He went down as if he'd been kicked by a mule.

He lay there stunned.

The others turned, startled, and Hawk went for his gun, then froze as he found himself facing Slocum's Colt.

"Just forget it, Hawk."

Hawk moved his hand away, shocked at Slocum's speed of draw.

Gordy shook his head, then pushed himself painfully to his feet. "What in hell did yuh hit me for?" he growled, rubbing his jaw.

Slocum pointed to the mark the bullet made in the wood. "Next time you shoot, mister, better hit what you aim at."

Gordy's eyes slipped to Curly, then back to Slocum. His face twisted. "Sorry I missed yuh, cowboy. I'll try again soon."

Slocum's green eyes were icy. "Of course, I could put a bullet in you right now, and then I won't have to worry about you trying to shoot me in the back."

Gordy paled. "You wouldn't shoot an unarmed man. It's murder!"

"That's what you just tried on me, you mangy mutt. Now git."

Gordy's face looked sullen with anger as he stomped out of the saloon.

Higgins and the other drinkers came up to Slocum. Higgins's face gleamed with pleasure.

"Slocum, it did my heart good to see you in action. That dog was shootin' at you, not at Hawk. A set-up, Slocum. They're out for you. For some reason, they're trying to stop you." His face looked grim.

"Because you stand between them and takin' over this town."

"They're not trying to take over the town, Higgins. They got something in mind, but it ain't the town."

"What is it, then?"

"That's what we gotta find out," Slocum said quietly.

He was riding south, toward the Gaines ranch, when he saw Lulabelle. She sat on a high smooth rock, which gave a magnificent view of the flat land and the towering mountain. It was in a way a striking picture, a beautiful girl alone in all that vastness, alone but fearless, enjoying the spectacle of nature.

He thought of how she had deliberately triggered the fight with Hardy and shook his head. She was a dynamite woman, plenty hot to handle.

He continued on the trail and soon forgot about her.

But, after riding on for ten minutes, it didn't take him long to discover that someone was tailing him— none other than Lulabelle. Why she was doing it was a mystery, but he didn't like anyone trailing him, so he doubled back and got behind her, easy to do.

She looked annoyed at having lost sight of her quarry, and stood on a high piece of ground, searching the landscape.

Still, when he stepped out behind her, from low brush, she didn't show surprise. She stayed calm and smiled coolly.

"You're not an easy man to nail down, Slocum."

"Why should you want to, Lulabelle?"

She studied him. "Can't blame me for trying."

"*Why* are you trying?"

She had cool dark brown eyes, long dark brown

hair, a pouting mouth, and the lines of a thoroughbred filly. It hardly seemed possible that she could be related to a squirt like Rusty. She touched her lips with her finger. "I'd like to apologize for the way I turned Hardy onto you. That was mean."

He grinned. "Mean is what makes you so endearing, Miss Lulabelle."

She gave him a mysterious woman smile. "You find me endearing, Slocum?"

His eyes gazed appreciatively over her body. "I reckon most men do."

"If that's the case, why'd you run from me just now?"

"Didn't run. Don't run from anyone. I was on my way to the Gaines ranch."

"You take quite an interest in the Gaines girl. Perhaps you find her endearing, too."

"Almost as much as you."

She stood there looking at him, her full lips in a sudden pout. "You talk an awful lot for a man of action."

That hit him. He rubbed his chin slowly. "I do think you'd like me to make a play for you."

Her eyebrows raised. "Might not displease me. Seems to me you been wanting to do that for some time."

He grinned. "A mean woman brings out the mean in a man." He reached out to her, pulled her body tight against him, and kissed her. She had full ripe lips, and she pushed hard against him; he felt her warm loins and her full breast.

Then she pulled away. "You're a bold, bad man, Slocum. *Too* bold."

That surprised him. He thought she'd be a hot-blooded playmate. His flesh had been fired, and he already had visions of making hard passes at the sexy body he'd seen naked in the stream.

"A man can never be too bold, Miss Lulabelle."

She looked off into the distance, then turned back to him. "Let's just say that I find you a mighty exciting man, but I'm fighting my inclinations."

He scowled, thinking that she was a tease. Then he felt amused. "Why fight them?" he asked.

She smiled. "You may find this a bit unexpected, but my father would like to talk to you."

He studied her. "Are you the messenger?"

She shrugged. "No. He just happened to mention that it would be nice to have a chat with you. He said he had invited you to the ranch a couple of times, but you seemed shy about riding in." She toyed with a gold bracelet around her wrist. "So, when I saw you, I thought I'd repeat his invitation." She glanced at him with seductive eyes. "Why not come out to the Bar H with me?"

He stroked his cheek. It was true that Hogarth had invited him twice. But he was not ready to go. Perhaps it had to do with his feelings about Rusty, even about Lulabelle. But he was feeling different now about her. Fact was, he was feeling horny about her.

"What's your dad want to talk about?" he asked.

She looked cool, always looked cool. A lady with a lot of self-control.

"I reckon he thinks you're a hard-riding, two-fisted, fast-shooting cowboy. He likes to have men like that around him. And, if he likes a man, he puts no limit on what he pays." Her eyebrows went up archly. "When I like a man, I don't put out limits either. A chip off the old block."

It sounded natural enough. Hogarth was a big land-owner, a cattle baron, and he was grabbing up land. Probably wanted top men, especially with the kind of gunmen floating around Dawson, to protect the Hogarths and protect their property.

"I don't rent myself out," Slocum said.

She looked thoughtful. "Why don't you listen to his proposition anyway? You might work out an arrangement." She smiled. "It's being said that you have the fastest gun around here. It might be worth a lot to let it be known that your gun is on the side of the Hogarths."

His jaw hardened. "I'm not a hired gun, Lulabelle. Appreciate the nice things you have said. I just do what I have to do to defend myself."

Her dark eyes shone shrewdly. "You are one tough customer. Wonder how I could persuade you." She started to unbutton her blouse.

He watched, fascinated.

Her breasts, pear-shaped beauties with pink nipples, came into view. Her eyes gazed searchingly over his body, her pouting lips smiled wickedly, and she ran her pink tongue over her lips.

He felt his male flesh almost jump. He watched as she slowly tossed aside her blouse, unbuttoned her jeans, and stepped out of them. He'd seen her body once before, but from a distance. Close up now, she was a splendidly built woman. Her body combined delicacy of line with sensuality: the fine modeling of a slender waist and rounded hips, finely structured thighs and legs. And the lips between her thighs peeped at him with shameless invitation.

His flesh swelled and his pulse pounded. "You sure know how to send out an irresistible invitation, Lulabelle." He slipped out of his clothes and moved to her.

She put up her lips for kissing, and again he felt them sweet as ripe plums. The touch of her breasts against his body made him tingle. When she took hold of his pulsating flesh, he sizzled. He kissed her breasts, caressed the curve of her back, her rounded buttocks, delighting in the silken feel of her skin.

Then, as she kissed his ear, she murmured, "There has to be a way of persuading you, Slocum." And she slipped to her knees, kissed his fierce flesh, and brought him into the depths of her mouth. It was a sudden, overwhelming sensation. With almost rapacious movements, she made love to it, her lips moving with clever, dynamic skill. He felt great waves of pleasure as she went on and on until, fearful that she would bring him to sudden ruin, he withdrew. She spread her thighs to receive him and he buried himself in her.

She sighed deeply. Then, whipped a by a fever of lust, he plunged in and out, feeling great waves of pleasure until it seemed his nerves sharpened to one shattering moment and he went off. She squirmed and twisted and her body went into convulsions of pleasure. Then she went still.

They lay together in a state of dreamy bliss.

The rifle shot echoed off the rocks, and the bullet seared his flesh.

He rolled off her, reached for his gun, always nearby, and pulled her to the shelter of an outcropping rock.

But there was no more gunfire.

He put his hand behind him. His butt had been nicked and the blood felt sticky.

He cursed. The bullet, he figured, had come from

the high ridge of rocks to his left. The damned bush-whacker must have been watching, but seemed to have had the decency to wait until the end of their game.

But to shoot a man at a time like that you had to be one low-down hyena.

His gun was ready, but where was the target? He looked at Lulabelle, at her impassive face as she calmly put on her clothes. She seemed almost unconcerned about the danger of another shot. Maybe she figured nobody would dare shoot at her, the daughter of Luke Hogarth.

Then, for just a second, he saw the rifleman up on the ridge, scrambling behind the boulders, probably for his horse. A flash, then he was gone.

Slocum waited, then went to his own horse, took a cloth from his saddlebag, and clamped it over the wound. The bullet had seared off a small piece of flesh. He cursed; a hell of a place for a wound. He had just glimpsed the rifleman, an unfamiliar figure.

Why? There could be no answers yet.

She gazed at him as he held the cloth against his butt.

"Now you must come to the ranch. We'll fix you up properly."

He shrugged. He would go. Though it wasn't a serious wound, it was a jolt to his pride. Humiliating. He'd like to get his hands on the low-down skunk who'd shoot a man at a time like that.

Slocum painfully slipped his jeans over the wound. He felt a bit fatigued from the blood loss, especially after his vigorous workout with Lulabelle.

"Let's go then," he said, "to your ranch I feel lousy."

Her lips were firm. "I can't tell you how sorry I am about this. Why are they shooting at you, Slocum?"

He climbed painfully over his saddle. "I been the target of someone ever since I hit this miserable town. If it's the last thing I do, I'm gonna find out why."

She smiled. "Like they said about you, Slocum, you're a two-fisted, stout-hearted fightin' man." Then she added slyly, "And you sure know a thing or two about lovin'."

The Hogarth ranch was an eye-opener. Slocum was prepared for a king-sized ranch, but not for the acres and acres of land, the corrals of cattle and of horses, the well-built ranch house and bunkhouses.

Hogarth was a cattle baron in the real sense of the word; he sent his cattle herds up the trail to Abilene.

Hogarth was leaning on the corral fence watching a cowboy putting the Bar H brand on a roped calf. When he saw Slocum ride in with Lulabelle, he grinned broadly.

He spoke to a cowhand nearby, who then started for the house. Hogarth came forward and shook hands heartily with Slocum, and smiled at Lulabelle.

"This little girl, Slocum, can do anything. Now, early this mornin' I made mention that nothin' would please me more than to see Slocum come ridin' up over that hill. She never said a word, but here you are. She's the most persuadin' little girl I ever met."

Slocum wondered if Hogarth had any idea of his daughter's persuading tricks. "Lulabelle does have her ways, Mr. Hogarth."

"I never refused that girl anything," Hogarth smiled. "She gets what she wants. S'pose that might spoil her a little. But what's the use of havin' all this if you can't spoil your young 'uns?'"

Slocum thought of Rusty, who put himself above the rules of civility. And of Lulabelle, who probably never denied herself anything. He glanced at her, so casual, cool, neat in her blue shirt and blue jeans; you would never suspect she just finished off some steamy sex.

"I ran across Mr. Slocum out on the range, Dad. Someone took a potshot at him. Sliced him a bit."

Hogarth turned quickly, his face concerned. "I'm sorry, Slocum. Are you hurt? Need a doctor?"

"It's just a scratch. Already stopped bleeding, I'm sure. Some hyena shooting from the ridge nicked my tail." Slocum's teeth clenched. "Like to get my hands on him."

"Did you see him?" Hogarth asked. "I'll put some of my boys on it."

"Waste of time by now," Slocum drawled.

Hogarth shook his head. "Musta been some of that scum that's drifted into town, doin' all the shootin' and killin'."

A Mexican woman came out with a whiskey bottle and glasses, which she put on a wooden table nearby. Hogarth led Slocum there and poured two glasses.

"I'm going to freshen up," Lulabelle said, cool as ice, and she walked toward the main ranch house.

Slocum watched her walking, graceful and erect. The jeans fitted perfectly to her elegantly rounded butt.

"A beautiful girl," Slocum said.

Hogarth nodded. "Everyone thinks so." He held a filled whiskey glass out to Slocum.

"I'm sorry you got shot. These gunmen have

knocked off a couple of ranchers. I'm concerned." He
lifted his glass and his grey eyes narrowed. "The only
man who seems able to stand up to them, Slocum, is
you. That's why I want you on my payroll. I need a
fast gun. I've got a big investment here." He smiled
grimly. "Just takes one bullet to wipe it out. Happened
to Lem Comstock and Archie Brown. I don't cotton
to the idea of tangling with one of the gunmen."

"Do you think they're an organized bunch, Mr.
Hogarth?"

"No. It's just random killing. Quick quarrels, quick
shooting—that's it. But it's dangerous to have men
like them hanging around." He stroked his chin. "I'd
like to make you an offer. Join my outfit. You won't
have anything to do. We'll spread the word that you're
working for me. Can't help thinking all that shootin'
might come to a stop. Don't believe there's a gunman
out there who'd want to come up against you."

Slocum pulled out a havana and lit it. "I'm not
sure, Mr. Hogarth, that my name would stop the
shooting. More likely, it'd start it. They been shooting
at me from everywhere. Someone's trying to wipe me
out."

Hogarth scowled. "Can't imagine why. You don't
even live in this town." He poured another drink and
gulped it. "Maybe you got an enemy. Would it be
likely that he'd be on your tail?"

Slocum shrugged. "There could be kin to a man
I've shot. You can't overlook something like that."

Hogarth leaned back in his chair. The grey eyes in
his broad, handsome face gazed with friendliness at
Slocum.

"I sure wish you'd join us. We got too few good
men. Rusty, of course, runs the outfit. Not because

he's the best—he's not—but he's my son. And he's smart. What do you say? You wouldn't have to take orders from him. I can tell you're a proud man, Slocum. I'll pay you fifty a week, and if you're forced to use your gun, there'll be a bonus of fifty dollars each time. What d'you say?"

Slocum looked at the corral where a rider was breaking a bronc. About seven cowboys on the fence were watching and jeering.

Something about one cowboy caught at Slocum's mind. He was rangy and rawboned; Slocum felt recognition, but couldn't place him. Did he know him from Georgia? The army? Kansas, when he rode with Quantrill? It bedeviled him.

Rusty came of the big house, walked toward them, and gave Slocum a friendly nod. "Glad to see you here." He turned to his father. "Did you sign Slocum up, Dad?"

"Just about to. Was telling him that he'd be a free agent. He'd run free of you."

Rusty scowled but said nothing.

"What about it, Slocum?" Hogarth asked.

"Let me think about it," Slocum said. "I don't like the idea of being a hired gun."

"You'd just be doin' what you're doin'. Cleaning out a rotten nest."

"I don't like to make up my mind in a hurry about a thing like this. I'll get word to you in a day or two."

Rusty nodded. "I suppose you should hurry. Dad likes to get everything very clear." He looked at his father, and Slocum was startled by the tinge of dislike that flitted in Rusty's eyes. "Dad doesn't like to gamble."

Hogarth's features became stern. "Only fools gamble, Rusty. I been trying to teach you that for a long time."

Hogarth turned to Slocum. "See, by hiring a man like you, I reduce the odds that the Hogarths and what they own is goin' to get hurt. Now, that's not gambling. That's judgment. Join us, Slocum. You won't be sorry."

The soft grey eyes gleamed in the ruddy handsome face, and Slocum felt the magnetism of Hogarth.

Slocum stood. "I'll have an answer in a day or two."

Hogarth's smile was genial. "Two days could be too late. Anything could happen. Think about it and let me know quickly."

Rusty stared at his father, and again Slocum sensed the current of antagonism.

He shook hands with both men and walked to his roan. When he mounted up, he glanced at the corral.

The men were still watching the bronc busting, all except the rangy cowboy. He was looking at Slocum, and when their eyes locked, the cowboy turned to the bronc.

Slocum rode off the Hogarth ranch with his mind bedevilled. He kept trying to fix the rangy cowboy in a time and place. He felt a vague excitement about it. Who was he?

His mind ranged back to the War. Was he a comrade in arms? It had often been his experience to find faces, familiar but unrecognized, belonged to Confederate men he'd known. But, try as he might, he couldn't pin down where this cowboy belonged in his past.

He tried to reach down to his feelings. Did he pick up the cowboy as friendly or hostile? He found them blurred. A bit hostile, perhaps. That made him more determined than ever to put a brand on this man. He sensed it was important. That cowboy also felt recognition; why otherwise would he be the one man to look at Slocum as he was riding off?

Well, somewhere and somehow he would run into the cowboy, and then he'd clear it up plenty fast.

It was useless thinking about it anymore. He would just run in circles.

To distract himself, he gazed at the land. It was June green and lush, the cottonwoods standing sturdy, the leaves sprouting thickly, the mountains huge against rose-colored clouds.

At a small stream, he stopped to let the roan drink, his eyes restlessly searching the land. He couldn't let his guard down for an instant, not in this territory. His butt ached. It had been lucky the bullet had creased the flesh high on his butt. Otherwise, riding could have been more painful.

He pulled off the bloody cloth and replaced it with a clean one. The first gush of blood had stopped and there seemed to be a small seepage now.

He gritted his teeth in rage. Bushwhackers—he hated men like that above all. Gutless dogs who didn't have the nerve to come out and face you straight, but worked in the dark, behind the brush. Backshooters were the lowest form of life in the West.

He rubbed the roan, and the horse turned his dark, gentle eyes on him and nuzzled him roughly. Slocum ran his hand affectionately over the muscled flank. The roan had stamina and heart, and had carried him through many a tight, dangerous spot.

He rode toward town while he thought about the

Hogarths. There was tension between the son and the father. Why? Maybe Rusty didn't like some of the old man's decisions.

Did Hogarth feel all that threatened? He had enough guns on that ranch for all the protection needed. Slocum wondered suddenly if Hogarth had deliberately sent his daughter out to bring him in, one way or another.

Maybe something was going on. He sensed something. It was a feeling, nothing more, but Slocum did not discount such feelings.

Why did Hogarth want him? Just because he was a fast gun? Could there be other reasons?

Hogarth felt that money could turn Slocum into a friend. Did he want to pull Slocum's teeth? What could he fear?

Well, Hogarth could fear that he might suddenly lose Rusty. He had to know that Slocum had knocked Rusty on his tail in front of Bryan's Saloon, and that Slocum had demanded explanations from Rusty about mysterious attacks from drifters and gunmen.

So this could be Hogarth's way of immobilizing a potential enemy. You brought him to your side with money. Hogarth was a money man; he would believe money could buy anything.

Slocum suddenly went rigid.

It was a thought, not the sight of danger, and the roan, startled by the sudden tension of his rider, pranced a few steps. Slocum pulled hard on the reins.

Now he placed where he had seen that rangy cowboy. Just a glimpse, yet it had been enough to fix the man's frame in his mind. He had been *the ambusher, the man who'd shot at his tail.*

But if it had been him...

A flow of thoughts surged through his mind. A man shooting at him and working on the Hogarth ranch.

Why was it that every time there'd been bullets or fists against him, it all seemed to come from the Hogarths? And yet, until now, he'd never had a clean, clear tie-up.

Even this rangy cowboy was not that clear. He might have shot at Slocum because he had a passion for Lulabelle and hated the man who had the luck to nail her.

It didn't necessarily link the Hogarths to the attack. He could be a solo gunman, activated by jealousy. Maybe a freak who didn't like to see loving couples. There were men like that.

No, he still didn't have convincing proof. Everything was hints or half-hints.

Besides, why would the Hogarths want him wiped out? He was not a threat to them, not that he could see. He had done nothing to justify vengeance from them.

No, this rangy cowboy, this bushwhacker, also looked like a red herring.

He sighed; too much to figure out.

The best he could do was try to pick up this bushwhacker somewhere, in town maybe, and squeeze the truth out of him.

8

The late sun was starting down in the buttermilk sky and Slocum had stopped at a water hole to let the roan drink when he saw the cowboy riding southwest. The shape of the rider looked familiar and Slocum studied him for a few concentrated minutes, then realized it was Hawk, one of the card players at the saloon, part of that phony gunfight. It was a gunfight, Slocum realized, whose bloody intent was to plant him in boot hill.

With a jaundiced eye, Slocum watched Hawk ride. His direction was southwest, and that was a puzzler: it was away from Dawson, away from the ranchers, and toward Santa Fe. Hawk rode as if he had a clear fix on his destination.

Slocum thought about Hawk for a few moments.

A mean-looking hombre, a hired gun; it should be extremely interesting to know where a man like Hawk holed up.

Now that Slocum thought of it, this was the first time he had had the opportunity of tracking one of the gunmen who had been ripping up the town of Dawson. Tracking Hawk might clear up a lot of mysteries about why the gunmen had stopped in Dawson, why they were killing, if the killings were chance encounters or not.

Slocum's jaw hardened; it might lead him into the lion's den, but it was worth the risk of finding a few answers.

He swung over the roan and started to track. It was easy; he let Hawk move out in front while he kept back so as never to be visible. The land was tricky with open patches of sand, boulders, and brush. From the tracks Slocum could read a rider not in a hurry who knew his destination. The trail seemed to be an old Indian one leading into a secluded area surrounded by dense trees. From the high ground, Slocum spotted a log house in a clearing. Four horses were tied to a rail.

His eyes narrowed. It would be nice to find out what the hell was happening down there. This could be a hideout for the gunfighters. If Hawk did hole up here, why not his card-playing buddies, Curly and Gordy?

But it would be dangerous to crawl down to that stinkhole after a lot of hard-nosed hyenas. If he made a mistake, their bullets would turn him into a sieve. It wasn't a smart idea, but it might be one quick way of solving the mystery of the gunfighters. Why were they here? Was there any rhyme or reason to their killings?

He picketed the roan back out of sight, then started down, moving soft-footed, staying behind cover. Slocum had learned the secret of survival in the territory: never give a bushwhacker a clear shot.

He came down slowly, with the patience of an Indian, finally reaching a thick tree trunk about twenty feet from the cabin. The grass at his feet was thick, there were strips of fallen branches; he had to be careful.

Voices floated out from the log house, but the distance muffled their meaning. He wanted to eavesdrop, then quietly make his way back. Just a stray sentence or a man's name might give him what he wanted.

Then he heard the high-pitched voice of a woman and gritted his teeth. A woman could concentrate their attention; they would scarcely talk business.

The voices were blurred, but it was too dangerous to move closer, and the presence of the woman discouraged him. He might just have to make the laborious trip back. Then he heard the hissing at his feet and, in haste, he sprang back from the rattler only the length of a step from his foot. The splintering of the branches under his feet did it, and three men with guns drawn were on the porch of the house staring at him.

"Get your hands up, mister," said Curly.

"We got a visitor," said another man.

"It's Slocum come to pay us a friendly visit," said Hawk.

"That's right, men." Slocum smiled genially. "Got

lost, saw the house, figured I might bunk here for the night."

Curly grinned. "Oh, you'd like to bunk for the night. I think we can put him up. What d'ye think, men?"

"Why not?" said Hawk. "He's a nice friendly cowboy. But he wasn't very nice to Jed and Burt."

"Sounds like a mighty dangerous fella. Better get his gun," said Curly.

Slocum didn't like that. He'd be helpless without the gun, but he couldn't try a shootout. They were too many. He cursed the reptile and reached for his gun.

"Take it out gently, by the barrel, with your fingers, Slocum," Curly said. "Good. Now just toss it over here."

He threw the gun.

A busty red-haired woman in a violet dress came out on the porch. "What have you found, boys?" she asked.

"Found this polecat sneakin' around, Emily."

"Was just lookin' for a place to bunk out for the night, ma'am. Saw the cabin, thought I'd scout it. Didn't know if anyone was here. A Comanche, maybe."

Curly looked at her. "Do you believe that, Emily honey?"

She looked at Slocum, a lean, handsome, powerful man. "He doesn't look mean-faced to me. Might be telling the truth."

Curly grinned. "You never could resist a good-looking man, Emily. All right, Mr. Slocum, just come right in. We'll put you up for the night."

Slocum smiled. "You're a mighty hospitable man, Curly."

Hawk grinned, too. "You can even have your gun back. Pick it up."

Slocum nodded, his heart jumping, and bent quickly for the Colt. Hawk was just as fast. Slocum scarcely felt the butt of the gun against his skull. The light just turned out in his brain.

The first thing Slocum became aware of was the pain in the back of his skull. He could hear voices, but they sounded as if they were under water. He kept his eyes shut, but his hands felt numb. He felt a powerful desire to shake them, but he could not move. Through slitted eyes, he could see that his wrists were tied. There had to be a knot on his head as big as a doorknob, the way his head felt. He cursed silently; this mean town would be his undoing. They had shot his butt, beat his brains, and now he was trussed like a turkey, ready for killing. And all for what? To find the man who killed the father of Cassie Gaines. Did she have any idea of the battering he was going through for her? These men were outlaws. Given the smallest excuse, they'd kill. He had to wonder if they wanted to kill him or not. At the saloon, he was convinced that they had a game going with him as the target.

Could he be wrong? He might have made a mistake. Otherwise, he'd not be breathing now or thinking about it.

He focused his attention on the voices. Only two men and Emily.

She was talking. "I don't know why you think so

much of Lulabelle Hogarth, Hawk. She seems meaner than a copperhead to me."

"Yer just jealous, Emily, honey. Just 'cause you ain't got a fine pair like she's got." Hawk laughed. "Don't you agree, Jaggers?"

"Oh, I think Emily has a fine pair, too," said Jaggers. "But that Lulabelle, she looks like she'd give a man a mean ride. I mean bust him wide open."

"And what's lackin' in me, Jaggers?" Emily complained. "Seems to me you been mighty content with the kinda lovin' you been getting around here."

"You're all right, Emily. But I'm getting sick of staying here. Hawk, I'm telling you the truth, I'm ready to shake the dirt of Dawson off my boots. We oughta move on, and to hell with the others, if they wanta stay. What d'ye think, Hawk?"

"Just between us, I'm getting tired, too. Just holed up, not bein' able to go where we want without permission. Now we got Slocum here. Don't know why Curly didn't finish him off." Hawk sounded disgusted.

"Curly can't make a move by himself."

Hawk grunted. "Slocum tracked me here, I'm sure of it. He's dangerous. He's the fastest draw around, I'll tell ya. Mowed down Jed and Burt at one time. D'ya know how fast you gotta be to shoot like that?"

"Yeah," said Jaggers. "Let's make sure his hands are tied real good."

"Oh, they're tied. And he looks like he's gonna sleep like an angel for another hour."

Then Emily spoke. "He's kinda nice. Don't know why you didn't believe he just stumbled here."

"I jest tole you, stupid, that he tracked me here," Hawk snarled. "He's a keg of dynamite. And we better get rid of him."

There was silence, and Slocum was almost tempted to open his eyes when Jaggers spoke.

"Can't do anything till Curly comes back to tell us what's what."

"Tole you, I feel nervous as long as he's breathin' and close by," Hawk said. "We don't have to wait for Curly. We'll say he tried to break free and we hadda shoot. What about that?"

"All right," said Jaggers. "If Curly don't get back in another ten minutes, I'll agree to that. Now I'm gonna stretch my legs. You stay put."

"He's tied tighter than a dead pig in a store window. Goin' nowhere. I want a stretch, too," said Hawk. "Emily, you make coffee."

Slocum heard the men go through the door and opened his eyes. He was lying in the corner, his body turned to the wall. Emily was standing at the stove, starting to make coffee.

Softly, Slocum reached his fingers down to the inside of his boot for his hidden throwing knife. He lifted it noiselessly, glanced at her again. She was busy at the stove, pouring water into the pot. He put the rope against the keen edge of the knife. The rope fell apart. Noiselessly he opened and shut his hands to restore the circulation. They had not tied his legs, figuring the blow on his head would keep him out. Curly had gone to tell someone that Slocum was ready for killing. Curly had to clear it, it seemed. That meant someone out there was giving orders. Rusty? And yet, he still had no real proof. But these two polecats, Hawk and Jaggers, weren't going to wait for a go-ahead from Curly, they said.

Slocum kept his hands together as if they were tied. The knife was in his palm.

Emily suddenly looked at him.

"Oh, I thought they had finished you, you were so quiet," she said.

"I got a real bad headache."

"It was Hawk. He hit you hard."

"Not a nice fellow. What are you doing here, Miss Emily?"

She smiled. "Man needs woman. That's what I'm doing here."

"But nobody here's your particular man, is he?"

"If he pays, he's my particular man." She smiled.

"Glad to hear it. Why are they here?"

"Don't know. They never talk business around me. Don't know a thing about them. They just want to have fun."

He smiled at her; she seemed to like him. "They plan to kill me, don't they?"

She looked solemn, but said nothing.

"Where's my gun?" he asked.

"Hawk's got it in his belt." She bit her lip. "I'm sorry you're in this fix. I'd help you if I could, but they'd kill me. They're killers."

He nodded. "Thank you, Emily. You're a good person. Why don't you go out the back way, on the porch for a time."

"Why?"

He looked at her. "You're nice. Don't want you hurt."

She stared at him a moment, felt something, then nodded. "I'll get some air back there." She went quietly out the back door.

He waited, his senses keyed up; there was a slim chance, but it would be a matter of timing. He heard footsteps outside the door. His body was mobilized. He held his hands together as if they were tied, the knife still in his palm.

The door opened and Hawk came in first. Three steps behind him was Jaggers. Hawk smelled the coffee and turned to the stove. He partly faced Slocum. Slocum's hand went back and the knife flashed through the air and buried itself in Hawk's chest. His eyes seemed to bulge out of their sockets. He was in shock.

Slocum sprang after the knife, held Hawk's body in front of him, pulling Hawk's gun from its holster, bringing it up. Jaggers had his gun out and fired, hitting Hawk. Slocum fired. His bullet struck Jaggers' forehead and he went staggering back as if he'd been poleaxed. He fell against the wall.

Slocum pulled a deep breath into his lungs and bent over Hawk, pulled his own gun from the gunbelt, put it into his holster.

He poured the coffee into a tin cup, not even looking at the two dead men. The coffee was hot. He liked the taste of it.

He took another deep breath.

Dawson—it was one hell of a town.

And coming here had been a waste. He hadn't learned a damned thing, just found out that some of the gunmen had a hideout.

But someone out there was giving orders. That was something to think about.

He'd give Emily some money, tell her to haul her behind out of here. He'd make tracks himself.

Yes, Dawson was one hell of a town.

9

Next morning, after a hearty breakfast of eggs, bacon, biscuits, and coffee, Slocum had mounted up and was riding toward the end of town when to his astonishment he saw Jesse Gray, his old riding pal with the Quantrill boys, walking into the barber shop.

Jesse Gray! Slocum remembered Hawkins saying that Jesse came to Dawson sometimes to visit his mother, who lived near the river. Jesse, Slocum had heard, rode now with one of the most feared train robbers in the West, the Jake Mercer gang.

Jesse was a big-hearted cowboy, and he'd been a true friend to Slocum. It would be a real pleasure to see him. He rode quickly toward the barbershop.

Jesse was sitting in the chair, a sheet around his neck, and Hawkins was staring with fiendish pleasure at his unruly shoulder-length hair. "I'm gonna commit a work of art on that god-awful mess, Jesse, that you allowed to grow on your head."

"I been saving this head of hair for your butchering, Hawkins."

Slocum stepped into the barbershop. "Ain't no other barber got the guts to cut the hair of Jesse Gray."

Jesse swung around and Slocum saw his six-shooter peering from under the apron.

"Don't point that iron at me, you thieving rascal," Slocum said.

Shock appeared in Jesse's blue eyes. Then he rose from the chair and flung his arms around Slocum, his face bright with pleasure.

"Blast your Georgia hide, John, if you aren't a sight for sore eyes." He stood back and surveyed Slocum. "Damn you, you haven't changed a bit. Still look like the hottest gun in Dixie." He pumped Slocum's hand. "It's shore nice to see you in one piece. Still manage to stay outa trouble?"

Slocum shook his head. "They're trying to shoot my butt off, Jesse. But I'm hanging tough. One day, I reckon, a bushwhacker's bullet is gonna catch me."

Jesse grinned. "The only place you're gonna catch a bullet, Slocum, will be in a bedroom." He dropped back to his chair. "I'm goin' to sit here while Hawkins butchers my hair."

Slocum smiled. Jesse looked like he had in the old Quantrill days. A dark handsome face, high cheekbones, luminous blue eyes, looking a little less wild now, and a powerful body. He'd been a fast gun and a deadly rifleman, and together, Slocum and Jesse had done a lot of damage.

Afterward, Slocum remembered, when things

calmed down, Jesse had stayed too wild, craved excitement, and joined the daring Jake Mercer bunch. Jesse was wanted in four states, and there was a thousand-dollar reward on his head. When he came down from Kansas to visit his mother, he skirted the towns, but made the exception in Dawson, dropping in to see Hawkins, who had also ridden with Quantrill, but turned respectable as a barber.

Slocum couldn't help thinking of the old days when he himself was wilder and harder. They were all young firebrands, ready to give their lives for the glory of the South.

Then came the ruin and the revenge of defeat. The life of the plantations, the grace and beauty of the old ways had gone down in the flames of Atlanta, in the bullets at Gettysburg, the wreckage at Antietam.

There had been no place left for men like him. That was why men migrated west, to a raw, rich territory where, if you had guts and stamina and a fast gun, you could survive, might even make a new life. Some men carved out a future, some a fortune, some a tombstone.

But not Jesse Gray, and not John Slocum. The scars of the war had gone deep for them.

Slocum gazed at Jesse's image in the mirror as thoughts of the past raced through his mind. After the War, Jake Mercer had gathered fighting men around him and formed a wild bunch. They did crazy things, robbed banks and trains, but tried to avoid violence.

"So how's Jake?" Slocum asked.

Jesse nodded. "Still the smartest brain I ever met for figuring out how to rob a train. Long as he's alive, we're in good hands." Jesse looked sober. "If we ever lose him, the bunch will break up."

Slocum looked at Jesse's boots, fine costly leather; his jeans were fine cords. He looked good, but his life could only end one way. "You look prosperous, Jesse."

Jesse smiled. "The money is in two places: banks and trains. Won't be long before they'll have the railroad goin' through here, Be able to visit Ma more often."

Slocum laughed. "They'll build a railroad through Dawson so your ma can see you more often, is that it?"

"That's it."

In the silence Hawkins concentrated on snipping at the long, unruly locks that grew down to Jesse's muscular shoulders.

Some thought simmered at the bottom of Slocum's mind and he stayed silent, waiting for it to rise while he watched the nimble fingers working the scissors.

When Slocum spoke, his voice was quiet. "Jesse, did I hear you say the railroad would be going through Dawson? Did you say that?"

"That's what I said, Slocum. Comin' through here, followin' the river, goin' on down to Santa Fe."

Slocum's eyes narrowed. "Do you know this as a fact, or are you just bulling?"

Jesse's blue eyes were cool. "Never bull, Slocum."

"But how'd you know a thing like that?"

"Jake tole us. He knows. It's his business to know. He has leads in Chicago, where they laid down the plans. Money's down on it. The railroad will come through Dawson and head toward Santa Fe." He grinned. "And some people in this town are gonna find themselves suddenly rich folks. Those with land near the river."

Hawkins looked up from his cutting. "That'd make Cassie Gaines a rich lady, wouldn't it?"

Slocum had already thought of that. "Who else owns river land, Hawkins?" But even before the answer, Slcoum knew who it'd be.

Hawkins paused in his cutting. "Sam Walker, Archie Brown, Lem Comstock. They useta own it. Pushin' daisies now."

"They seemed to have run into sudden bad luck, all of them," Slocum said.

An ironic smile twisted Jesse's lips. "Funny kind of coincidence."

Hawkins wasn't listening, just cutting hair.

Slocum was thinking about what Higgins had told him. That Luke Hogarth was a kind-hearted man, a pillar of the town, and mighty generous to the widows of those dead landowners.

Kind-hearted Hogarth.

It came together in Slocum's mind, the bits and pieces of the puzzle.

The gunmen who mysteriously drifted into Dawson. But they didn't *drift* in, they were *drafted* in. Hired guns. And their job was damned clear: make an occasion to find, fight, and shoot certain landowners. Then Luke Hogarth, the only man with enough cash, would step in, this kind-hearted pillar of the town, and give a generous settlement to the widows. And take claim to the land, which he said, of course, that he didn't need.

But he needed it all right. Because he knew that when the railroad men came, they would give big money for the rights to build on that land. And because Hogarth had been so kind-hearted, he would come into a fortune.

See how virtue is rewarded in Dawson, Slocum thought.

From the beginning, he had been trying to understand why he had become the target of violent men. The reason, he now saw, was because he'd been trying to solve the Gaines killing, to clear himself in Cassie's eyes.

But if his search for the killer was successful, it might lead to the Hogarths. Not Luke directly, of course. But to one of the gunmen, working under Rusty.

It was odd how all the clues kept pointing to Rusty, but that he had cleverly, somehow, always managed to blur the evidence.

Now things were clearer.

This last ambush with the bushwhacker working on the Hogarth ranch was another piece of evidence.

What about Lulabelle? Was she part of the scheme? Did she put him in a position to get picked off, use her body as a lure? Was that possible?

At the beginning, Slocum figured, Rusty had just wanted revenge for getting manhandled. But when Slocum was discovered to be a fast gun, and interested in solving the Gaines killing, gunmen were put on his tail. Hawk, Curly, and Gordy, among them.

All with one aim: *Kill the man whose poking around could unmask the Hogarths*. But it didn't work. Slocum's gun was too fast.

Then Luke Hogarth, a clever man, changed the tactics. He would buy Slocum off, bring him onto the team, maybe keep him nearby until a chance came for some quick backshooting.

Slocum ground his teeth.

This Hogarth was a devil. Silky, soft-voiced, seemingly big-hearted, but underneath he was a scheming, greedy land-grabber whose towering ambition was behind the brutal killing of his neighbors.

Slocum watched Hawkins now shaving Jesse.

It was important to remember that Hogarth was a powerful man, and it would be dangerous if he got wind of Slocum's suspicions. For the time being, he'd move slowly, maybe warn Cassie Gaines, and wait for the right time.

Jesse looked at Slocum's reflection in the mirror. "You seemed bothered, John. Anything I can do?"

Slocum smiled. "You got enough, Jesse, to keep clear of the law. Just keep taking care of yourself."

Jesse grinned. "I keep clear of them and they keep clear of me. We got a understandin'."

"It's your fast gun, Jesse," Slocum said. "They got respect."

Hawkins grinned. "Remember Kansas City, when you two came outa Dugan's Saloon, and ran smack into six bluecoats marchin' down the street. Just the two of you. One of the bluecoats yelled, 'It's Jesse Gray!' That was the dumbest thing *he* ever did. They tried to get their rifles down for firin', but you boys were blazin' away, and the six of them were bleedin' in the street while you went for yore hosses. I saw it all from the stage depot. Then you-all came tear-assin' down, howling Dixie, and that street went clear quicker'n the blink of a bat's eye. Never figured how you did it. I mean, how come you didn't waste bullets, both shootin' at the same man?"

Jesse grinned. "Easy, Hawkins. I jest grabbed the three on my side, Slocum took the three on his. You jest knowed that sort of thing."

Hawkins shook his head. "The bluecoats never saw shootin' like that. Made them mighty respectful, mighty careful folk after that." He pulled the apron off and said proudly, "Think I almost made you look human, Jesse."

Jesse gazed in the mirror at his clean-shaven face and his shorn locks. "I'm feared Ma won't recognize her lovin' son." He turned to Slocum and put out his hand. "John, it's nice to see you again. If you ever want to make a piece of big money, let me know. Jake Mercer knows the kind of man you are."

Slocum shook his head. "Not my way of makin' money, Jesse. Take care of yourself, you buzzard."

Jesse smiled. "I never stop doin' that." He glanced out the window, looked both ways, his bright blue eyes suddenly icy, his hand near his holster. But he saw nothing threatening, and he walked out the door to his gelding tied to the hitch rack.

As he watched the gelding lope out of town, Slocum's mind whirled with thoughts.

The sun scalded the sky and a white glaze hung over the land as Slocum rode toward the Gaines ranch. Heat struck the earth mercilessly, and the grass and leaves seemed to wilt under the impact. Living creatures huddled in the shelter of shadows, as if yearning for the cool of the night to come.

Slocum let the roan drink at the river, and afterwards he wet its sweating haunches. His own body sweated; he stripped quickly, dived into the water, splashed about, then came out.

He was mopping his body when he caught a movement and flung himself to his gunbelt, grabbing his gun. But it was Cassie Gaines standing at a twist of the river. She had come to the shade of a thick gnarled tree, stared at him for a moment, then turned away.

He grinned; he had nothing to be ashamed of. He had a lean, hard, muscled body, and had never met a woman who complained about his main male feature.

She was probably walking toward her horse, picketed farther back. On such a blister of a day, it was natural for her to head down to the river, which marked the edge of her land.

Refreshed, he slipped into his clothes, swung over the saddle, and walked the horse toward her ranch.

She was sitting under a big oak with thickly branched leaves near the main ranch house. There was a pitcher of tea on the oak table with two glasses.

Her face seemed faintly blushed, the right expression, he thought, for a woman who'd just seen a man stripped.

"I'm sorry, Miss Cassie. I didn't know you were there."

She shrugged. "We live in a world of human accidents, Mr. Slocum. I was thinking of bathing myself. This weather is fierce."

He smiled. She always handled herself like a lady. A pity he hadn't happened on her swimming instead. Then he remembered his ferocious fracas with Hardy because he'd seen Lulabelle in the skin. Hardy had called him a peeping polecat. He would hate to get a brand like that.

"Have some tea, Slocum?" she asked.

He grinned. "A stiffer drink, perhaps?"

She stared impassively, then called, "Rita, bring out some whiskey." After a pause, "Seems a bit hot for whiskey, Slocum."

"Yes, but I don't drink tea."

She looked at the sky, then she mopped beads of sweat off her brow with a neat kerchief.

Rita, a young Mexican girl, brought out a bottle of whiskey, flashed her dark eyes at Slocum, and scampered back to the house.

"Help yourself, Slocum."

He poured whiskey into the glass and sipped it. She watched him with her lovely brown eyes, and again he found it baffling that a girl like her could find Rusty Hogarth interesting. A beautiful girl, she had high cheekbones, a delicate nose, a lovely modeled mouth, and full lips. Her golden hair cast a glow around her head.

"I s'pose you've come because you have news, Slocum."

He nodded. "Yes, I have news."

She leaned forward. "You found out something?"

"Don't exactly know who shot your father, but I've got some ideas."

She looked disappointed. "Ideas! I've got plenty of ideas. I want to know the killer, who did it. That's what I want."

He sipped his whiskey. "Before we get to that. You had been talking about selling your land. Is that what you're planning to do?"

She stared, puzzled. "What's that got to do with anything?"

"It's got plenty. I remember you saying you might sell and join your aunt in Fort Worth."

"No, I'm not going to do that."

He smiled. "Good."

She stared again. "I suppose I should be flattered, but I think you take a curious interest in my personal affairs, Slocum."

"As long as you don't sell."

She shrugged. "Don't need to sell. I've decided to marry Rusty Hogarth."

He was thunderstruck. In fact, his expression was so strange that she frowned.

"Something wrong with you, Slocum?"

"For God's sake, don't marry him," he said brusquely, and gulped down the rest of his drink and poured another.

Her beautiful face became stern. "Mr. Slocum, you must be the rudest man I ever met. Who gave you the right to say that? My personal affairs do not concern you." She stood up.

"Maybe you better listen to me before you go." His voice was cool.

Something about him impressed her. She sat down, her face pale.

"First, I'd like to say that I've heard that the railroad is going through Dawson. Right on your land. So, if you hold onto your land, you could become a rich woman."

She looked astounded. "How do you know that?"

"Told you that I heard about it, from someone reliable."

She gazed at him while she digested what he'd said.

"I reckon," he went on, "that I'm not the only one who's heard about it."

She had been thinking deeply, then turned to him. "And what does that mean?"

"I think the Hogarths know."

Her eyes narrowed. Then she said, "I'll have some of this after all." She poured whiskey in her glass, drank it, and waited for him to go on.

"I think the Hogarths have known for some time." He paused. "And if you know what the Hogarths are like, I think you could judge how they might act."

Her lovely mouth went tight. "I don't know what you mean. Luke Hogarth is one of the most generous men in Texas."

"May look like that. But you've heard of the wolf in sheep's clothing. Who do you suppose owns the land on the river? None other than Luke Hogarth. You have to ask how'd he come by it? Four dead ranchmen: Comstock, Brown, Walker. Looks like he's gonna get the Gaines land through marriage. It wasn't necessary, after all, for them to eliminate Bill Gaines. That was a mistake. But Luke Hogarth doesn't take chances."

Her face turned white. "Are you trying to tell me that my father was shot by Luke Hogarth?"

"No. He didn't do the dirty work himself. He's got hired guns for that."

Her face was hard; her eyes glared with anger. "How do you know all this?"

"Look who owns the river land—Hogarth."

She studied him. "And that's your reason? Just that?"

"Listen. Ever since I got here and crossed Rusty, I've been shot at, manhandled, bushwhacked. Why?

Because I was trying to hunt down the killer of your father."

She glared. "Tell me this, just this: who told you a railroad is coming through Dawson? *Who* told you?"

She was not going to believe a thing unless he offered her something solid, but he couldn't name Jesse Gray.

"A man who rode with me during the Quantrill days. A friend."

She digested that slowly. "Quantrill. God, he was the craziest, the worst killer of them all. You're asking me to take the word of a gunfighter about a decent, generous man like Luke Hogarth?" She stood up, her face hard. "You always made slurring remarks about Rusty. You bad-mouthed him without reason, just like Tim Blake did. I'm disappointed in you, Mr. Slocum. Your dislike of Rusty seems to have poisoned your judgment. Maybe you're just plain jealous of him. Whatever it is, I don't want to listen to you any more. I'd like you to leave my land." Her face was pale with anger.

Slocum felt a flash of anger. Why was he knocking himself out for this woman? He had tried to solve the killing of her father, and all he got for his pains was a lot of fighting and shooting, and a lot of sass from her. Why go on? It wasn't even his business. If she was dumb enough to marry a sneaky pipsqueak like Rusty and live with a family of hyenas like the Hogarths, then let her. To hell with her.

"Miss, it's your funeral," he said calmly, and walked slowly to the roan. As he rode off, he glanced at her face; she looked pale and grief-stricken.

The roan cantered down the western trail, and the

sun, a ball of orange, sat on the majestic peaks of the Sierras.

As Slocum rode, he made the decision to leave Dawson.

But he didn't like the sour taste of it all.

10

Now Dawson was behind him. The roan cantered southwest, and Slocum looked at the massive mountain pitching its spires at the washed blue sky.

A lone eagle rode the wind on its mighty wing span and Slocum watched it. He could feel its loneliness. He, too, traveled the great spaces of the territory alone. But he didn't mind; it was always other people who made things go bad. Give a man his horse and his gun and an open sky above him.

So why did he still have this bitter taste?

It was mostly Cassie Gaines. She had shot at him in the mistaken belief that he had killed her father. The main reason he stayed in Dawson was to help her. And gunmen came out of the woodwork to try to shoot his head off.

He had to use his gun for defense, but he had stayed

mostly for her sake. And when he found out who was doing the killing, she didn't believe him. She gave him the rough side of her tongue, told him he was poisoned by jealousy. Cassie Gaines might be beautiful, might be a gutsy filly, but she had to be a dunce. Any woman who'd fall for Rusty Hogarth had to be a dunce.

But that was how some women were; they could go crazy over some mangy dog of a man. It was a mystery.

The roan kept riding south.

To hell with Dawson, the Hogarths, their gunmen, the damned railroad, and, most of all, the stiff-necked Cassie Gaines.

He'd keep riding.

It wouldn't be the first time he had shaken the dust of a stinking town off his boots. He had to realize it wasn't his job to clean up all the rattlesnakes in the world. You couldn't do it, anyway. You clean up one, you'd find another crawling under a rock. Let Dawson stink in its poisonous juice. There was nothing to hold him there.

Then he heard the roar of the rifle and the bullet whipped the hat from his head. He dived off the horse flat on his gut as another bullet struck the dirt inches from his body. He rolled quickly to a half-buried boulder and slid behind it, cursing. He could see his hat twenty feet away with a hole through it. An inch lower would have splattered his brains.

This was it! The hyenas were trying to kill him, had just come a hair's-breadth away from it. Now he would not leave Dawson until he was finished—one way or another.

He had fought with Pickens on Round Hill, with death around him, fought in Kansas with Quantrill, fought up and down the raw territory, defending himself against redlegs, gunmen, drifters, desperadoes. He had come out scarred, battered, but never beaten.

And he wasn't going to let the mangiest hyena of them all, the bushwhacker, drive him out of Dawson.

He studied the land: rocks and ridges, boulders and brush. The bullet had come from the brush-covered ridge on his right. The rifleman had a sharp eye, and it would be dangerous to tempt another shot with a run to a nearby boulder. But he needed that shot to get a fix on the rifleman's position. His move would have to be sudden to force a quick shot, which he hoped would miss. He waited. And the bushwhacker waited.

The rock was eight feet away. The rifleman would have seconds to aim his rifle and trigger it.

Slocum gathered himself, hunched his body, and sprang for the boulder, his gun out, his eyes up. The rifle bullet whistled past his head as he dropped, yelling as if he had been hit. He was behind the boulder.

He had a fix now, and all he wanted was for that hidden skunk to put out an inch of his head.

He would do it; it was just a matter of patience. Most men, Slocum thought, considered themselves sharpshooters.

Sooner or later this skunk would believe he had scored, and rather than sweat for hours behind that rock, his patience would fade and he would edge out.

Slocum lay silently, without movement, waiting. It was the patience game, and the loser won death

He wondered if this rifleman would be the same

rangy cowboy who had trailed him before and shot
his butt during playtime with Lulabelle.

This had been a bad move by the Hogarths. They
didn't know Slocum had been fed up and was heading
out of town. If they'd known, they would surely have
called off their gunman and said "good riddance."
They had made a fateful move, which brought him
back into the fight.

He didn't care that much what Cassie Gaines thought
about him. She thought him jealous of Rusty. Well,
he'd help her in spite of herself. He'd pull the mask
off the Hogarths, show her and the town that far from
being a big-hearted cattleman, Luke Hogarth was a
low-down profiteer who had good men gunned down
for their land.

Slocum's thoughts kept him occupied while he
stayed alert to sound or sight from the vertical stone
block behind which he suspected the rifleman lurked.

He heard it, then: a rock scuttling downhill.

He didn't move an inch, just grinned.

The hyena up there was testing. He'd thrown a
rock in the belief that it would bring Slocum's head
up if he was alive.

But, if he wasn't, there'd be no movement.

No movement.

Slocum waited, his neck craned to listen. The man
with the rifle by this time had to believe Slocum had
been hit. His cry, the silence, the lack of movement,
especially when the rock was thrown.

There. A crunch of boot on pebble!

Slocum waited.

Another crunch.

Slocum brought his gun to the edge of the rock,

his finger on the trigger, and slipped one eye past the edge of his boulder.

The rangy cowboy was out in the open, hunched, taking a step down that forced him to lower his rifle. Slocum shot the arm holding the rifle; it fell with a clatter.

He tried to scuttle back to shelter, but Slocum shot his right knee, and he collapsed. He crossed his left arm to grab his pistol, and Slocum shot his left wrist.

He lay there with a busted knee and two wrecked arms.

Slocum came forward, his gun ready.

The cowboy just lay quietly. He looked up at Slocum, the whites of his eyes red, his lips drawn back to show his teeth. Then he looked at the blood pumping out of his arm and leg.

"I'm all busted up. Finish me off, Slocum."

"You'll live," Slocum said coolly, "if I get you to a doc. Who are you?"

"Jensen."

"Why were you shootin' at me, Jensen?"

The dark brown eyes looked into the distance. He had a lean, strong face, a high brow, a powerful neck, and his black hair flowed over his ears.

"Might as well finish me, Slocum. I'm not talkin'."

Slocum's smile was cold. "I won't finish you. Just let the starving coyotes feed off you."

Jensen held his busted wrist as if trying to stem the bleeding. The thought of the coyotes put a gleam of fear in his eyes. "Don't do that, Slocum. I had nothin' against you. Just following orders."

"Whose orders?" Slocum's face was hard.

Jensen looked miserable, but clamped his jaw. Slocum pulled his gun. "I'll break your other knee. That should keep you here tonight. Ever see starving coyotes at work, Jensen?"

The dark eyes brooded at the image. "Just shoot me, Slocum. Please. I'm not good any more."

"Seems to me you could have a lot of years if you stay on the right side of the law. You got one chance." He leaned down. "I'll make it easy for you. Was it Hogarth?"

Jensen shut his eyes, then nodded.

"Rusty Hogarth?" Slocum asked.

Jensen nodded again. "I'm dead for tellin' you. Nobody crosses the Hogarths."

"Maybe not, Jensen. I'll help you. Why do the Hogarths want me dead?"

Jensen's face was grim; then he shrugged, as if nothing much mattered any more.

"They been wantin' you dead a long time, Slocum. First because you whipped Rusty. Nobody does that to a Hogarth. Then because you were poking around too much, askin' about Bill Gaines."

Slocum leaned down to stare into the dark eyes. "Who shot Gaines, Jensen? Did you?"

"No, not me."

"Who did?" There was fire in Slocum's eyes.

"It was Rusty."

Slocum was startled. He hadn't expected it to be Rusty. It didn't make much sense. He thought a bit. "Why'd he shoot Gaines? He was planning to marry the daughter."

Jensen shifted painfully. "Gaines saw the Archie Brown shooting. Gordy had picked a fight with Brown and shot him. Gaines saw it. Rusty was there. So

Gaines demanded to know why Rusty didn't stop his man, Gordy. Said as far as he was concerned, Rusty was just as guilty as Gordy in that killing.

"Then Rusty very quiet said he was crazy 'bout Miss Cassie, and he hoped Gaines wouldn't stand in the way. Gaines tole him he didn't want a killer for a son-in-law. Rusty musta figgered he'd never get Cassie with Gaines alive. 'You accusin' me of being a killer?' he told Gaines. 'Now pull your gun.' And, before Gaines could bat an eye, Rusty shot him."

Slocum's face was hard. "How much does Luke Hogarth know about all this?"

Jensen grimaced. "He knows everything. He's behind it all."

Slocum saw the movement high on the ridge, and with instinctive speed ducked as the bullet sang past his ear.

A second bullet struck Jensen, ripping his chest. Slocum shot at the gunman, who slipped behind a crag; his bullet splintered the rock.

From his cover, Slocum looked down at Jensen. He was stone dead.

He looked up at the ridge. The gunman had slipped down behind it, presenting no target. Slocum stood motionless, listening. Then he heard the neigh of a horse. The gunman was going. Slocum had just glimpsed him: a bearded man, Gordy, the one who had shot at him in the saloon. He'd been sent by the Hogarths as a back-up man, just in case Jensen didn't get his man. Gordy had seen Jensen talking, and that had been enough. Hogarth men had been picked for loyalty.

Slocum stood still, a frown on his face. He had

the story now, from the horse's mouth. Most of it, he had suspected before, but this was cold proof. Cold was right, because Jensen was dead. Would Cassie believe his unsupported word? She would still think he was jealous of Rusty.

It didn't matter; he would go back to Dawson. He was tired of being shot at. It was a miracle that his skin was still whole. A piece of his butt was shot off, and his body was in rack and ruin from manhandling.

He was sick of it.

And the way to stop it was to hit the Hogarths, not their henchmen.

Could he do it by himself?

He was going to try.

At the Bar H, Luke Hogarth leaned on the corral fence as he watched Rusty trying to ride a wild bronc. The boy had guts, Luke thought, and he couldn't help feeling a touch of pride at the way Rusty stuck on, though the bronc kicked and heaved. Hogarth was mostly satisfied with his son, who was smart and gutsy, a chip off the old block. But Rusty had made a bad mistake.

Some time ago, Hogarth had told Rusty that Miss Cassie was the peach of the town, and that the stretch of the Gaines land would be worth a pretty penny. Rusty could do himself a lot of good by snuggling up to Miss Cassie. At that time, Hogarth didn't know that the Gaines land would be railroad land. He found that out later in a talk with banker Fletcher, up in Chicago. Fletcher told him the big secret, that the railroad people were going through Dawson, aiming to pick up riverfront land, and whoever owned it would become rich. Hogarth hated to hear that; he owned thousands of acres of fat, grassy land, but not an inch of it touched the river. He was consumed with envy. Luke Hogarth was an obsessed man, obsessed with being the richest and most powerful man in southwest Texas. He owned great herds of cattle and horses, but the railroad money would not be going to him, but to Gaines, Brown, Comstock, and Walker. These men had lucked into the river land, and Hogarth felt he'd been cheated.

Hogarth hated three things: poverty, weakness, and failure. When the War ended and the South went down, he didn't waste a minute lamenting the loss of the old ways, the grace and charm of plantation life. He departed with his young family from an Atlanta half-destroyed, in the hands of greedy strangers, and he went west. He fought Comanches, grabbed land, bought cattle with his wife's money, and, with driving force, he prospered. He was a sharp man, but clever enough to conceal it; in fact, he worked hard to give the impression of charity. When his wife died, thrown from a frightened horse, he shot the horse, but never shed a tear. He doted on Lulabelle and Rusty, and secretly nourished thoughts of a dynasty.

Hogarth was building for the future. He knew that, behind most fortunes, hard and terrible decisions had been made. He wanted that railroad land, and he could think of only one way to get it.

The route of the railroad was still secret, and he had to act fast. He told Rusty what had to be done, and because Rusty was cut from the same cloth as his father, he didn't lift an eyebrow. But he didn't like it and said so. Well, Hogarth himself didn't like it, but it had to be done.

Ten hired guns were brought in from New Mexico;

picked men, ready to be loyal to the hand that paid them. The gunmen would stay near Dawson till the job was done, then vamoose. The job? To quarrel with four landowners, demand a showdown, and shoot them.

Then big-hearted Hogarth would come in, with compassion and money, and help the widows, giving them a good price for the land. The widows couldn't operate the land by themselves, and they would never pass up his generous offer.

That had been the plan. And it had worked.

Except for Bill Gaines. That had been messy.

Bill Gaines saw Gordy deliberately insult Archie Brown and then shoot him. He thought it cold-blooded murder, and held Rusty responsible because Gordy was his man.

Then Rusty made an idiotic mistake in the belief that Gaines would stop the marriage between himself and Cassie. He shot Gaines. On top of that mistake, he made a worse one: he blamed Slocum for the Gaines killing.

A shout went up from the cowboys as the bronc, in a frenzy of heaving, finally threw Rusty. Rusty landed easy, got up, grinned, shook his fist at the bronc, then walked to the side of the corral.

Hogarth watched Rusty with his piercing grey eyes. He liked the boy, as much as he could like anyone, but Rusty had been stupid about Slocum. Rusty's pride had been hurt by Slocum, and he wanted revenge. He put one hired gun after another on Slocum, but he was a hardcase. Chances were Slocum would have just drifted through town if nobody had bothered him. But the attacks nailed him down, roused his ire, and, because he'd been blamed for the Gaines killing, he stayed put, determined to find out who did it.

Until Slocum, everything had been working out fine.

Miss Cassie was going to marry Rusty, bringing her land to the Hogarths. And Hogarth already had the other riverfront land.

But now Slocum stood like a massive block, spoiling Hogarth's plan. If Slocum ripped the truth out, the Hogarth dream of dynasty would vanish.

Early that afternoon, Hogarth had told Rusty to put Jensen on Slocum, to bushwhack him. And he told Rusty to send Gordy as a back-up, in case Jensen didn't make it.

Hogarth looked at the sun; it was low in the sky.

Where in hell was Jensen? What about Gordy?

Hogarth motioned to Rusty who lighted up a cigarillo and drifted over to the fence to join his father.

"That bronc is one mean critter, Dad. But I stuck with him, didn't I?"

"You did real good, Rusty."

Rusty gazed at his father, blowing smoke in the air. "You look worried."

"I am. There's neither hide nor hair of Jensen or Gordy."

Rusty nodded. "I know. I tole them to come right back."

Hogarth's grey eyes clouded. "It doesn't look good."

"Too soon to say," his son replied.

Hogarth didn't bother to answer. He looked at Rusty. "We better push ahead on Miss Cassie. We should have the ceremony tomorrow."

Rusty grinned. "The faster the better. Nothin' worryin' you, is there?"

Hogarth's jaw clenched. "Plenty is worrying me.

If Slocum ever gets one of our men to talk, there'll be plenty to worry about."

Rusty's face hardened. "They've been warned. They're all in it together. Any man talks, he's done for."

"Slip-ups happen, Rusty. When Cassie's your wife, our position will be strong. Maybe Slocum will give up . . . if he's still alive."

"Probably eatin' dirt right now, Dad. Jensen's a good man, one of the best trackers we have."

Hogarth's eyes were cold. "Slocum has mowed down our best men." He shook his head. "I always figured you a smart boy, Rusty, but you were a bone-head to blame Slocum for the Gaines killin'. Why'd you do that?"

Rusty looked grim. "He knocked me down, like I tole you, in front of the saloon. I don't think you'd want me to take that. You tole me plenty of times, nobody knocks a Hogarth around and lives. I figured two gunmen would take care of him, so I tole Jed and Burt to accuse him of the Gaines killin'. It would clear me and get rid of him. Seemed the right thing at the time, Dad. How could I know Slocum could shoot like that?"

Hogarth examined the face of his son. Who did he look like, this boy of his? Not his mother, who'd been beautiful, or himself. A throwback. But he was slick. "I s'pose it looked good at the time. No way you coulda known Slocum was such a fast gun. But you never shoulda shot Gaines. We could have won him around. That was the first bad mistake. The second was to blame Slocum. If we hadn't ruffled his feathers, he might have just gone riding out of Dawson.

He's the type who won't go till he gets behind the shootin'. That means us. He's dangerous as a cobra. We don't have much time. I been thinking we should use Miss Cassie to bring him into a trap. Don't let her know, of course, Meanwhile, you ride over to Miss Cassie and tell her you're a hot and impatient lover, and you can't wait to make her your woman. Women like to hear that."

Rusty grinned. "Happens to be the truth, Dad. I long to get that beauty into my bed."

Hogarth nodded. "She's a beauty. And she'll give us good-looking Hogarths. I want plenty of them. Rusty, I'm trying to build something. Someday the Hogarths are going to be the first family in Texas." Hogarth's face hardened, "And don't think it won't take blood and sweat. So, go on now, up to Miss Cassie."

Hogarth saw the bearded Gordy ride to the corral and tie his horse. Hogarth didn't like the look of him. He waited for Gordy to come close.

"Where's Jensen?" Hogarth's voice was hard.

"Dead." Gordy's mouth looked grim.

Hogarth stared at him for a long moment. "And Slocum? Is he dead?"

Gordy shook his head.

Hogarth looked off into the distance, his eyes cloudy. "What happened?"

"Slocum shot up Jensen, forcing him to talk. I saw it from the ridge." Gordy combed his beard with his fingers. "Jensen was spilling his guts. I took a shot at Slocum, then hit Jensen."

Hogarth studied him. "You missed Slocum?"

Gordy nodded.

"And you shot Jensen?"

"He was spilling his guts—it was clear as day-light."

"You did the right thing about Jensen. How'd you happen to miss Slocum? Why can't anyone hit that hyena?"

"He doesn't give you a shot. He never stands in the clear any time. And he's got the devil on his side. Always seems to know you're there jest before you shoot. It's devilish."

Hogarth shook his head. "He's just flesh and blood, and he'll bleed quick as anyone else. Did he get a look at you?"

"I don't think so."

"Don't *think* so. You don't know? And he's already warned you at the saloon. So eat and get off the grounds."

Hogarth watched Gordy slouch toward the bunk-house. He'd done the right thing, stopping Jensen. There were men who cracked under pressure. So Jensen had talked. That made Slocum more dangerous than ever. He was a deadly force that threatened every-thing Hogarth had planned for. There had to be a way of trapping him, catching him with his guard down. Cassie Gaines might be the bait. Slocum trusted her. He had to work out a scheme.

He was thinking about it when he saw Lulabelle. She looked smart as a whip, riding her big black stallion, dressed in her tight tailored riding pants, her English brown vest and short-brimmed black hat. Though Hogarth felt a tingle of pride, other feelings swept over him, too.

Lulabelle was like an unbroken filly. She'd been hard to handle as a child, and as she grew older, she became worse. She did whatever pleased her, and devil take all others.

She had a piece of his own devil in her makeup, so he could hardly fault her. He, too, had been cursed with wanting what he wanted. In his case, he had to work and scheme and sweat to get it. And get it he did.

But she got it all on a silver spoon, and was spoiled to the core. He admired her, the way you'd admire a tiger; but you could never tame it, and she was a deadly hunter. Well, he was no old-fashioned father. Anyway, he could never control her, but he could sometimes get her to do things for the family, if it pleased her.

He waved at her, and she bridled the stallion and brought him to the fence.

"Something on your mind, Dad?" she asked.

He nodded.

She swung off the horse and came close. She had glowing dark eyes and fine body lines, taut as a racehorse.

"What's going on, Dad?" she asked cheerfully.

"I tole Rusty he should speed up the wedding. Tomorrow, maybe. Keep yourself ready."

"Rushing it, are you, Dad?"

"Yes, we want to close the deal. We want the Gaines girl and the Gaines land."

Lulabelle slapped her boot with her whip. "She's a pretty thing, Cassie is. Rusty's mighty lucky. Don't know why she'd marry him." She looked coldly at her father. "He's such a pipsqueak."

"Don't talk that way about your brother. He's a smart boy."

"Not smart as you think, Dad. It's because of him

that we've got Slocum on our necks."

Hogarth stroked his chin. Lulabelle saw things just as clearly as he did, and he often thought it a pity that Lulabelle hadn't been his son; she was fearless, gutsy, smart as a whip.

"That Slocum is a ball and chain around my neck, Lulabelle."

Her eyebrows raised. "He's a lot of man. And there are too few like him in Dawson."

He scowled. "We got other things to think about, Lulabelle. I got reason to believe he may know a lot of what's goin' on."

Lulabelle grimaced. "That's unfortunate."

"It could be worse than that. We have to come down on him like a ton of iron."

"I've done my piece, Dad, set him up. Can't help it if your Jensen can't shoot straight."

"Jensen's dead."

Lulabelle's eyebrows went up. "Was it Slocum?"

"Slocum had nailed Jensen. And Jensen was shootin' off his mouth. Gordy shot him. Had to do it."

Lulabelle's smile was not nice. "So Slocum knows plenty."

"He knows, but he can't prove a thing. He'll probably go to Miss Cassie, try to stop the weddin'. That's where we got to nail him." He stared at her. "Is there something you can think of, Lulabelle?"

"What do you mean?"

"A woman can bring a man's guard down. You oughta know by now."

"Thanks, Dad. I know what you think of me."

His grey eyes became steely. "You keep doin' what you want. I haven't interfered. We need your help now. The family. You better start thinking of the family or you won't have any of this." He gestured around the ranch.

Her dark eyes gleamed. "I don't want to see his blood."

"He's gotta bleed to die."

Lulabelle looked at her father almost with distaste.

"Tell me what you want." Her voice was flat.

11

When Rusty rode onto the Gaines land, he couldn't help smiling with pleasure. It was rich, fertile land, stretching for thousands of acres, and it bordered the river, and that was what the railroad men wanted. The land was worth a fortune.

Rusty had to think himself a lucky fellow, not only because of the land, but the lady. Miss Cassie was beautiful, and there wasn't a man for a hundred miles around who wouldn't give his eyeteeth for a woman like her.

Rusty had a fine opinion of himself, but still he couldn't help thinking the main reason he had landed Cassie was because his name was Hogarth. Cassie might be beautiful, but she had a smart head on her shoulders, too.

She was riding a colt around the corral when she

saw him. She dismounted, and they walked together to the oak table near the main house.

"Let's have some whiskey to celebrate," he said.

"Bring out the whiskey, Rita," she called, then turned to Rusty. "What are we celebrating?"

"Our weddin'. It's gonna be tomorrow."

She smiled. "A bit quick. Aunt Flo is coming from Fort Worth and bringing some fine wedding clothes. Can't be married before then."

"I tell you, Cassie, I can't abide the waiting. You got a hot-blooded bridegroom here."

She smiled. "It's nice to know, Rusty, that your blood's all boilin'. But another four days of waiting won't burn you up."

He looked grim as the thought of Slocum flashed in his mind. "Never know—lightning could strike me down."

Rita brought out the whiskey bottle and glasses, and smiled broadly at Rusty. He looked zestfully at her full buttocks which moved with sensual rhythm as she walked back to the house.

Cassie picked up his glance and didn't like it.

Rusty poured the whiskey and she held up her glass. "I can see you're a lover in a hurry." Her voice was cool.

He bit his lip. It was stupid for him to reveal himself. The main thing was to marry Cassie; afterward, he could do as he pleased.

"I'm sorry, Cassie," he said, and poured another drink for himself. "I'm just a red-blooded Texas lover who wants his woman."

"Just as long as the woman is me, Rusty."

He lifted his glass and felt the whiskey burn. He

looked at Cassie, golden blonde, with a lovely face. How lucky could a man get? Tomorrow night, he'd have her in his bed, and his imagination leaped as he thought about it. But for now he had to keep a tight rein on his desires. Nothing must go wrong. He hated to have his father down on him.

"Know what I heard, Rusty?" she was asking.

"What's that, honey chile?"

"That a railroad's gonna cut through my land."

Rusty stared, thunderstruck. How in hell did she hear that? From who? It was the most guarded secret. Not even the gunmen knew, so they couldn't tell. All they knew was that certain landowners were to be taken care of.

She frowned at him. "Did you hear it, Rusty?"

He caught himself. "No. Course not. Just astounded. Never heard a thing like that. Why should a railroad come through Dawson? No, I hadn't heard a thing. Nor Dad either. He'd know a thing like that."

"That's what I thought."

Now in control, he grinned. "Who tole you such a cock-and-bull story?"

"Slocum told me."

Rusty's mouth twisted. Slocum, the devil himself. Where in hell did *he* hear it? How could he learn it? Only his dad, Rusty, and Lulabelle knew it.

Cassie was watching him.

"Slocum always bad-mouths me. Says the craziest things about me. Don't know why. Hates me. And I sure try to be friendly."

She nodded. It fit with her ideas. Slocum was jealous of Rusty, that was all.

"He said miserable things about you, Rusty. I hauled

off and let him have it. It put him in a terrible fret, I could see. Wouldn't be surprised if he's gone and left town."

Rusty's mind worked frantically. He'd sent Jensen and Gordy after Slocum. Damn! And he might have been on his way out of town. If they nailed him, that would be that. But if they didn't, it would turn him around, and he would come back hard. He was that kind of man.

Bad luck. His dad's instincts were right. Things were getting tighter. Cassie hearing about the railroad, Slocum knowing about it.

He poured another drink. To hell with it. He was not going to brood about Slocum. It spoiled the taste of the whiskey.

"Listen, to hell with Slocum. We're here to talk about a weddin'. Whatcha say we make it tomorrow?"

"All right, Rusty." She smiled teasingly. "As long as it's not my *land* you're after."

"Oh, I'm after you and everything you got," he said, laughing. "But I'm bringing plenty. What the Hogarths got."

"Yes, that's something, too, Rusty. I want to be honest with you. I like the Hogarths. Your father's a fine man, and I admire what he's done. I see the building of a great country, and we can be part of it. That's how I'm thinking. A girl's got to get married, and I guess you're the best pickings in Dawson."

He grinned. "And you're the prime peach of Dawson. So tomorrow's okay. We hold the weddin' here. I'll bring the preacher, Dad, and Lulabelle—just the few of us. Next week we'll throw a big party to celebrate at the Hogarth ranch, for your Aunt Flo and all the others."

She got up. "A great idea. Tomorrow it is. And, Rusty, you can kiss the bride-to-be."

He kissed her, and not long after he was riding back in a gallop to tell the good news to his father.

Early afternoon, and the land looked green and silent. The roan cantered at the sandy bottom of a steep, rock-littered hill, and Slocum's thoughts centered on Cassie Gaines. He would force her to face the truth about the Hogarths, one way or another.

The trail led up the hill. There was Lulabelle, practically striding it.

His piercing green eyes instantly swept the surrounding land, but he saw nothing suspicious.

She came toward him on her handsome black stallion, and he had no doubt this meeting was deliberate. She had staked him out on the trail to the Gaines ranch. Why?

He thought of their last meeting, and couldn't help grinning. Did she enjoy it so much that she had come to play again? She wanted what she wanted, but she was also a Hogarth.

Had she come for fun or for her father?

She brought the stallion closer. "Isn't this a nice meeting, Slocum?"

She looked sexy; her silky blouse was unbuttoned at the top to show plenty of breast. She swung off her stallion, clearly inviting him to stop.

Again his eyes swept the land—nothing. She was a beautiful woman, but the way a rattler was beautiful. The kind of woman who could love you and sting you to death. The last time she had put her arms around him, a piece of his butt got shot off. But it was hard to believe that she had set him up. As Slocum figured it, she had stopped him because she liked her sex, and to bring him to her father, who made an offer— join up or die. Why was she here now?

She was a sexy little minx and she liked men. If he encouraged her, she'd be doing something mighty pleasant in a few minutes. He felt his flesh harden, a surge of desire.

She was a Hogarth, and by now the Hogarths knew that he knew what they'd been doing to get the railroad land. In innocence, Cassie would tell Rusty about Slocum's suspicions. And Gordy, who had shot Jensen, would by now have told Hogarth that Jensen had spilled the beans.

That was why this sexy little devil was here—to cut him off, one way or another. He could play her game and enjoy her beautiful body, but he'd better make sure she had no gun to do damage. And, from the slope of this land, a back-up ambusher could work from that boulder pile to his left. If he was not there now, he could never get there without Slocum seeing him.

"It's nice meeting you, Lulabelle."

"I been missing you, Slocum. Hopin' you been missin' me a bit."

He came off the roan and walked toward her, facing the boulder pile. It forced her to turn to face him.

He gazed appreciatively at her body, trim, fit, full-hipped in her tailored riding pants. She was a lot of woman, and her luscious mouth was shaped for loving.

He felt himself bristling in his jeans and realized he was doomed to stop. It was dangerous, almost stupid, because she had to be a setup. Because of the man Hogarth was, because she had been waiting on the trail to the Gaines ranch, and because she'd picked a spot where a bushwhacker could work, it had to be a setup. It would be like making love under the gun, but he found the idea strangely exciting.

Her dark eyes gleamed with secret fire. "I'll tell you straight, Slocum, I been wanting you. Love the way you make love."

"You ain't so bad," he grinned.

"So why haven't you looked for me, Slocum?"

His green eyes were cool. "I don't think your kin is crazy 'bout me, Lulabelle."

"Why say that?"

"They been trying to kill me, that's why."

"Why would they want to do that, Slocum?"

"Because I know too much, Lulabelle."

"What d'ye know?"

"That Rusty had a couple of ranch owners shot."

Her expression never changed. "Men get shot in Dawson for just no reason at all."

"They also get shot just for their land, Lulabelle." A long pause. "So you think Rusty's trying to get you shot?" she asked.

He smiled. "Wouldn't be surprised if you were, too, Lulabelle."

Her smile was deadly, yet admiring. "Slocum, you are the most red-blooded man I ever met. Wish you'd come over to our side. We'll make you rich." She took a step closer to him. "And happy."

She had stepped between him and the boulders. Clearly she didn't care for anything to happen to Slocum just now.

"I don't care for rich, Lulabelle."

"How about happy?" She slipped to her knees and unbuttoned his jeans, as if she knew from the bulge that he was in a state of excitement. She brought him out, and he looked big, fierce, swollen with desire.

She sighed. "You're born to make a woman happy, Slocum." And she kissed it, up and down, did some tricky things with her tongue, then engulfed him in the warmth of her mouth. She cupped him, made love to him, seemed to go wild with passion. She moved her lips fast and furiously for a few moments, then, like an obsessed vampire, she seemed to be devouring him as his passion zoomed, and she brought him almost to an explosion. Then suddenly she stopped, pulled down her riding pants, and brought him over her, spreading her thighs. He slid into the depths and the warmth of her, and she groaned as his hips moved with frantic fury. She suddenly screamed as he swelled mightily and fired.

"Oh, God," she moaned.

There was a dramatic pause, and she lay quietly for a while. Then, as she came around, she did a strange thing, raising her right arm straight up. Slocum, aware of danger, lifted her as a gun barked. Her body, in front of him, caught the bullet, and she jumped. Slocum's gun, already in his hand, fired blindly at the boulder. His bullet made the bushwhacker duck for cover. Slocum glanced at Lulabelle; the bullet had hit her shoulder, and she fainted from shock.

Slocum waited. The bushwhacker, with his gun out, peered from behind the boulder. Slocum shot his gun and he jerked his hand as if he had touched a hot branding iron.

Slocum came forward. The gun lay on the ground, ruined by his shot. He stopped twenty feet from the boulder. "Come out with your hands up. If I have to come after you, you're dead."

The bearded man came out, his hands up, his mouth taut. Slocum recognized Gordy, the man who had tried to shoot him during the card game.

Slocum stared at him, cold-eyed. Gordy squirmed, looked toward Lulabelle, biting his lip. "Did I hit— is she dead?"

"It's her shoulder. You're a rotten shot. Where's the nearest doc?"

"Doc Willard. His place is three miles west of town."

"I'm taking you, Gordy."

"Where? The Hogarths will . . ."

Slocum's face was grim. "Don't worry about them." He put his gun on Gordy. "Move."

When he got back to Lulabelle, she was still lying quietly, her face white, her eyes open.

"You'll live," he said grimly. "Which is more than you wanted for me."

She bit her lip. "I'm sorry, Slocum. You may not believe it, but it's not the way I wanted it."

His face was impassive. "I believe it. I'm gonna take you to Doc Willard. He'll get the bullet out."

Slocum pulled a leather thong from his pocket and tied Gordy's wrists. "We ride to Doc Willard, then to the Gaines place." His voice was hard.

"What do I do there, Slocum?" Gordy asked.

"Nothing much. You just tell her what you know about her father's killing. You were there."

"You must be loco."

Slocum swung his fist at Gordy's jaw, and he went down like a toppled steer. He shook his head, trying to clear it. Then he said, "That's brave, hitting a man with his hands tied."

Slocum's green eyes were icy. "I'll not only hit you with your hands tied, but I'll string you up. I know what you've done. You've got one chance, and that's to tell the truth to Cassie Gaines. Keep that in mind."

Gordy blinked, but said nothing.

They rode toward Doc Willard's place, Gordy leading the way, his hands still tied, Lulabelle sitting in front of Slocum on the roan.

"You'll be all right after the bullet comes out," Slocum said.

She turned to look sideways at him. "So you're going to tell Cassie Gaines all about the dirty Hogarths."

"That's right. Don't want her to get caught up with a hyena like Rusty."

"Got a soft spot for Cassie, haven't you, Slocum?"

"She's a nice girl."

"What does a man like you want with a nice girl? You need a woman like me, Slocum."

"Yeah, like I need a rattlesnake."

"You don't need a pale-faced, thin-blooded filly like Cassie Gaines. Why not be smart? Join us, the Hogarths. We're goin' to be the first family in Texas."

Slocum just looked ahead, stony-faced.

Her eyes flashed fire. "You're wastin' your time. Cassie and Rusty are already married. You're too late to bust up things. So why don't you just ride off and leave us be?"

He grinned. "You Hogarths have tried to kill me 'bout half a dozen times. Now you're asking me to ride off and let the man who killed Bill Gaines marry his daughter, a young lady I happen to admire. Thank you, missy. Just be happy you're still breathing after the things you tried to do."

They came in sight of a nice stone house with smooth green acres, Doc Willard's place.

After they dismounted, Slocum tied Gordy's feet with a leather thong. "That should keep you put. I'll be right back."

He carried Lulabelle to the front porch. Doc Willard, a small, neat man with glasses, came to the door and stared at Lulabelle.

"Doc, I'm John Slocum. Miss Lulabelle had an accident. Bullet in her shoulder. I'll leave her with you. Got some rush business."

"Bring her in, Mr. Slocum."

When Slocum came out of the house, he gazed at the sky. The sun was moving toward the horizon. He untied Gordy's feet.

"Let's ride." His voice was hard as iron.

12

Hogarth watched Preacher Wilson as he performed the ceremony.

"Do you take this man to be your lawful wedded husband?"

"I do." Cassie spoke in a low voice.

Hogarth, standing back, scarcely heard the question put to Rusty. He was thinking that he'd been clever, and that all his schemes had worked out. He had told Rusty to court Cassie and, like a good son, he did. Now the Hogarths had the Gaines land, and it would be the richest in southwest Texas. The railroad men would pay a fortune for it and for the other land he owned now.

Everything had worked out real smart.

"I pronounce you man and wife," Preacher Wilson said.

Hogarth's jaws clenched. There—it was done. No man, not even a man like Slocum, could put it asunder. If Slocum was still alive.

He glanced north. Why hadn't Lulabelle showed up? They had gone ahead with the marrying without her; it was important to put the Hogarth brand on Cassie. But he felt nervous about Lulabelle. Neither she nor Gordy had showed up. He didn't like it. That Slocum was a devil. Well, he might already be stopped. Lulabelle was a clever girl; she'd do what had to be done.

He glanced at Rusty. Rusty was glowing. He kissed Cassie. "Well, you're Cassie Hogarth now. And don't you forget it."

She smiled and looked at Luke Hogarth, who beamed at her. "Must say, I'm proud to join your family," she said.

Hogarth kissed her cheek. "Welcome to the family. We're just at the beginning, Cassie, honey. We got big ideas—ideas big as the territory of Texas. And you're gonna be right in the middle of it."

"Sounds excitin'. If only Dad could be here on a day like this." Her eyes brimmed with sudden tears.

Hogarth nodded solemnly. "Think of me as your dad, Cassie. You'll never want for anything in this world, long as I'm around."

He gazed at Rusty, who grinned at him like a son who'd done the right thing.

"Wonder what's keeping Lulabelle?" Cassie said.

"Maybe she's got horse trouble. Wanted to take a run toward Secaucus Springs before she came here. Gordy is with her. She'll be here." He stared out at the rich green land, and the sparkling river at the edge.

"Rusty and me are gonna prowl your land a bit. Might pick up some ideas how best to use it."

"You both go ahead. I want to see how Rita is doing about dinner."

She and Preacher Wilson watched them ride off together, father and son, and she smiled at the sight.

Preacher Wilson took her hand. "Miss Cassie, you did a right smart thing, marrying into the first family of Dawson. You can expect big things from Mr. Hogarth."

"Thank you, Preacher."

She watched him ride off, then she stood looking at the sky, which was beginning to flame red and orange. She loved to see the sun sink down and glow in the river. A hawk was flying at high speed through the sky, and far off, the mountain gathered a purple crest of clouds around its peaks.

Though she felt happy, there was also an undercurrent of foreboding. She wondered where it came from. Suddenly she realized that it came from Slocum, from what he had said about the Hogarths. An outrageous, unbelievable thing to say. It had to come out of jealousy of Rusty. Jealousy—yet before he said those terrible things she never would have believed him to be jealous or small-minded. What did it prove? Just that you couldn't know a man that easily.

Rusty—did she really know him?

She smiled; perhaps you never knew a man until you slept with him. She thought of Rusty, then of Slocum, and shook her head. Slocum was all man, and fascinating, but he had a bad streak in him. Not a man for settling down. He had the wanderlust in his eyes. She wanted a man who could strike roots and build for the future. Why did she think about Slocum at all. She didn't like the way her mind was working.

Then a movement of two horses on the horizon caught her eye. It shocked her to recognize that one of the men was Slocum. Just thinking of a man sometimes produced him—such was the mystery of things. Why the devil was he coming here now? she wondered grimly. On her wedding day. She studied the man riding with him. She'd seen him on the Hogarth ranch—one of the cowhands.

She frowned. His hands were tied.

What on earth did it mean?

She looked south, the trail the Hogarths had taken. They were nowhere in sight.

As Slocum rode closer, the foreboding that lurked deep in her mind seemed to move more to the surface. She almost dreaded his approach. He rode as if he were one of the horsemen of the Apocalypse.

What did he want? What was about to happen?

Fear coursed through her body. She waited, her heart thumping.

Slocum pulled the reins of the roan and jumped off. He had his gun out, and motioned roughly to Gordy, who dismounted clumsily, because his hands were tied.

She scowled. "What's the meaning of this, Slocum? I told you you are not welcome on my land."

His face was grim. "I understand how you feel, Miss Cassie. But *I* gotta do what *I* gotta do. After that, *you* can do as you please."

Her lips tightened, and she said nothing.

He pulled a havana from his chest pocket and lit it. "I heard that you were going to marry Rusty today."

"Who told you that?"

"Lulabelle."

Her eyes opened, amazed. "Where is she? She was supposed to be here."

"She's getting a bullet dug out of her shoulder by Doc Willard."

Cassie frowned and stared at him silently. "What happened?" she finally asked in a low voice.

"She tried to stop me from coming here. She used her charms, and this polecat used his gun. He shot her instead of me."

Cassie's mouth twisted. She couldn't make sense of it. "I'm sorry Lulabelle got shot. I hope she'll be all right. But what's this got to do with me? Why do you persist in coming here when you know you're not welcome?"

"You want to know why?"

"Yes, for God's sake. Why?"

He paused. "I don't want you to marry the man who shot your father."

Her face paled. "If I had a gun, I'd run you off my place. But Rusty, whom I have already married, will be here soon. He'll do it."

"You married him?" Slocum's voice was quiet. He shook his head, stared at her almost with pity, then turned to Gordy. His voice was hard. "Go ahead, Gordy."

Gordy stood silent, a dark flush on his face.

Cassie's eyes narrowed. "What are you doing here, Gordy? With a man like him?"

"It's the truth, Miss Cassie, what he says." Gordy's voice was low but clear. "Rusty did it. Shot your dad. I was there. I saw it."

She stared at him, open-mouthed.

"I had just shot Archie Brown. We had a squabble. I started it. I was paid to start it, by the Hogarths. They wanted three men dead: Brown, Walker, and Comstock. I got Brown. Your dad saw it. He was there. He blamed Rusty for not stopping the killing. Said that Rusty was just as guilty, because I worked for him. Then Rusty asked Gaines if that meant he'd stop him from marrying you. Mr. Gaines said then he wanted no killer for a son-in-law. Then Rusty said, 'You called me a killer. Draw'—and he shot the old man. That's how it happened, Miss Cassie."

Cassie had listened to him when he started with hostile eyes, but as he continued, her face became agonized. When he had finished, she seemed to be in shock.

She looked from Gordy to Slocum, and back to Gordy. Her mind raced. She almost didn't want to believe him, but she knew it was true. It had to be true. There was something that she had picked up from Rusty, something like a dirty little secret locked deep in him.

Why did they do it? Why? Was the railroad story true after all? All the men killed were river-land owners. *And Hogarth did have the land.* The killings had stopped—no further need of them.

And her father: they didn't mean to kill him; it had been an accident. He happened to be there when Brown had been shot.

Otherwise, they just planned to use Rusty, the most eligible man in Dawson, to get the Gaines land. Now she was married to the man who had killed her father.

It was a horror.

The thought burned in her mind. It was impossible. Why did they want such a fast marriage? Because they feared Slocum and what he knew. Slocum, whom she had cursed and accused of jealousy.

He had been her friend, all this time.

She staggered a bit, and Slocum, who had been watching her, moved close. She leaned against his chest and tears welled up in her eyes.

Gordy bit his lip.

Slocum felt a great sorrow for her, and put his arm around her shoulder.

She stood like that, silent.

Finally she said, "I know what I must do."

He studied her. She looked desperate. She might do the wrong thing.

"Tell me. I'd like to help."

An ironic smile twisted her face. "I'll do it. I know what must be done. Rusty is my husband." Her eyes went hollow.

Slocum stroked his chin. "I'll be close by. Just outside. Just in case."

Cassie went into the house, poured a glass of whiskey, and sipped it. Her face taut, her eyes hard-set, she stared at the glass in her hand. She wasn't seeing the glass, but her father, a kind, loving man who never raised his hand against her or said a harsh word. A handsome, jovial man whose deep brown eyes were like her own. After he was gone, she found that each time she saw the reflection of her eyes in the mirror, he came vividly into her mind. After her mother's death, he had been mother and father to her. His death had ripped her apart; she was good at concealing her feelings, but part of her mourned him some part of every day. In this territory, however, you lived on the edge of death, and you had to go on no matter what.

And so she had picked up her life. She would go on with living. And what was the main event in her life? Marriage. And marriage to whom? To the man whose bullet had destroyed her father—that kind, loving, wonderful man.

How did this rotten dog of a Hogarth dare to approach her with the offer of marriage? To dare to think of putting his bloody hands on her. He had come to her not out of love, but out of greed for land.

She took quick gulps of air, as if her fury had made breathing difficult. She raised the glass, drank all the whiskey, and felt the burn in her throat.

She would prepare herself. She washed, combed her golden blonde hair, used a flower-fresh scent.

Then she waited.

Time passed, she didn't know how much, but finally she heard the hated voices, the son and the father.

"Hey, Dad, I'm goin' to pay my respects to Mrs. Cassie Hogarth," Rusty said in a jocular voice.

"All right, son. I won't be far."

Rusty whistled as he went into the house, moving to the door of the bedroom. He had seen acres of beautiful land, great for cattle, even greater for railroad tracks. His father had told him they'd be rich beyond their wildest dreams.

He would have all this. And throw in the most beautiful woman in South Texas—Cassie.

He opened the door and smiled.

There she was on the bed, her hair finely combed, her face glowing; she looked ready for love, and he ached to give her some. He saw the whiskey bottle on the bureau, poured himself a drink, and downed it.

"You look mighty pretty, Cassie."

"Thank you, Rusty." Her voice was low. Probably shy, he thought.

He could see her pink breast, its fullness under the transparent chemise. He felt stirrings.

"D'ye mind if I pay a husband's respects, Cassie, honey?"

"No, Rusty, I don't mind." Her voice was husky, low. *She's eaten up with passion,* Rusty thought zestfully. He pulled off his jeans, his boots, and slipped under the covers.

He turned to her, breathing hard.

Her eyes were glowing, her skin looked lovely. He'd never seen her look so beautiful. She smelled like fresh flowers. Damn, was he a lucky cowpoke. He put his arms around her.

"Rusty."

"Yes, honey."

There was a long pause, and he looked at her.

Her eyes looked strange, fierce almost. "You shot my father, didn't you, Rusty?"

His face drained white and he felt himself suddenly go empty. He'd never seen a look like that in her face. It sent a shiver down his spine. "Who tole you that terrible thing?"

She was staring at him; she already knew from his expression.

"You did it, didn't you." Her voice was relentless.

The blood had drained out of his face. She knew; somehow she had found out. There'd be no point in denying it. It wouldn't wash.

"He called me a killer, Cassie. And he was going to stop our marriage. He gave me no choice. It was a fair fight."

"Oh," she said, "it was a fair fight. Kiss me, Rusty."

He gazed at her in shock, then delight. This beautiful woman believed him, had forgiven him. And now she'd give him her body.

He leaned forward to kiss her.

The sound of a muffled gunshot filled the room. Rusty fell back against the pillow. He put his hand to his side and looked at it. It was bloody.

Somehow he got up, stumbled out of the room, and found himself face to face with his father, who had heard the gunfire and came rushing in.

"What happened?" he demanded, fear in his eyes.

Rusty was holding his left side, as if trying to stop the loss of his lifeblood. "She shot me," he said. "For her father." He paused, looked at the blood in his hand. Then his face hardened. "She was right. I deserved it. And now I'm gonna die. And for what? For your dirty, rotten land. It was you behind it all. You greedy old man." He stopped. "And now I'm finished."

Hogarth looked destroyed. "Rusty, what are you saying? I did it for us—for you, for Lulabelle. You'll get it all."

Rusty stared at him. "I didn't want to go through the blood. I tole you that."

"There was no other way," Hogarth said.

Rusty staggered. "It's all over. Doesn't matter."

Slocum appeared in the doorway. He heard Rusty and caught him before he collapsed.

Hogarth, in a daze, looked at Rusty, now dead. "Rusty, my son, my boy, my boy . . ." he sobbed. Then he turned on Slocum. "It was you, always you. You're the dog who destroyed everything." He pulled his gun.

Slocum, still holding Rusty, stared in helpless shock.

A pistol fired and Hogarth staggered. He turned to look at Cassie, standing in the doorway, her gun still smoking.

He fell, crawled painfully to Rusty's body, and died beside him.

13

Several days had passed since the death of the Hogarths. It came as a shock to the town that Luke Hogarth, seen as a big-hearted man who loved to help his neighbors, was instead a secret land-grabber who with his son commanded a bunch of hired gunmen.

Overnight, the threat that hung over Dawson seemed to melt away. The small remnant of gunfighters, deprived of boss and of money, just drifted out of Dawson.

The town settled back to its peaceful ways.

Slocum, too, felt that his job in Dawson was done, and was ready to ride on.

He saddled up and rode out to say goodbye to Cassie Gaines. It was a beautiful June day with a washed light blue sky, a balmy sun. The land looked fresh and vibrantly green, the insects chattered and the birds sang.

Cassie Gaines looked more than usually beautiful. Her golden blonde hair in the glow of the sun seemed to give radiance to her creamy skin. "I won't offer you tea this time, Slocum," she said.

There was a bottle of whiskey and two glasses on the wooden table set in the shade of the leafy oak.

He poured liquor into both glasses.

"I s'pose we ought to toast your future, Miss Cassie."

"What kind of toast?" She took up her glass.

"You'll be the richest lady in Dawson. We could drink to that."

"Money isn't everything, Slocum."

He smiled. "Like the man says, it'll do till something better comes along."

They drank, then were silent for a few moments.

She grinned suddenly. "Something special came in the mail from Chicago today, Slocum."

"What was that?"

"A silky nightgown. My wedding-night gown."

He gazed at her. "Are you sorry you won't have occasion to wear it? I feel personally responsible for having deprived you of your wifely pleasures." He sipped his drink.

She sighed. "A girl's life is a hard life without a man, Slocum."

"I'm a man."

She looked off, her eyes clouded. "Oh, yes, you're a man. Nobody has dared to question that. But not a man to stay put."

He felt a wave of gloom. It had looked for a moment as if something interesting might happen, but not any more. She was not a woman for a traveling man.

She stood up and stretched with sensual grace. "Come in the house, Slocum. I've made an apple pie, a new recipe. Like to get your opinion of it."

She went through the door of the house to the living room. He followed, gazing at the movement of her hips. She had a slender waist, a full pair of hips—a woman's body. He lamented that he'd never know her intimately.

As if she sensed his stare, she turned. "I can't help feeling you're a passionate man."

That astonished him. "Why do you say that?"

"Your eyes burn with feeling."

"That's because you excite me, Miss Cassie."

She shook her head. "If a woman were to give herself to you, it would leave her with a lot of grief after you went off. You're a tumbleweed."

He sighed. "She might have good memories."

She smiled. "Yes, she might have that, at least. And memories are something not to be lightly passed by."

He looked hopefully at her. Her full lips were pursed, and he had never seen a woman more desirable for kissing.

She patted her golden hair. "I never did rightly thank you for all you have done. I s'pose there's no way I could." She gazed at him thoughtfully. "Do you mind if I kiss you, Slocum?"

He was astounded and managed to gasp, "No, I don't mind."

She put her mouth to him, her eyes closed.

He kissed her. Her mouth tasted flower-fresh. He could feel her breasts against his chest, a womanly body pressing against him. A surge of passion took hold of him. They stood there, tight against each other.

He dared not take his lips from hers; he could feel the smoldering of his flesh ignite hers. Her body tightened, and the warmth of her loins was firm against his hardened excitement. She seemed suddenly to be clutching him as tightly as he did her.

He pulled back for air.

Her eyes were still shut. She seemed to have sunk into a trance of passion.

She waited.

Again he put his mouth against her firm, full velvet lips. She was delicious to kiss. His hand gently touched her breast. She did not shrink. His hands caressed her over and over, then went behind her, to her back, her buttocks. He could feel her straining against him.

A searing desire swept over him to possess her. His hand went to the button of her shirt, opened it swiftly, and he caressed the creamy breast, kissing her again.

Then he stooped to put his tongue to her breast. Soon she was sighing with pleasure. He unbuttoned her shirt. She had perfectly formed breasts, lovely shoulders, a moulded neck that supported a beautiful face.

"You're beautiful," he murmured.

She gazed at him, her eyes glowing with unmistakable passion. She took his hand and led him to the bedroom. They were naked within a minute. Her body was put together with symmetry, the slender waist widening into shapely hips; she had firm, rounded thighs and finely formed legs. Golden hair shyly covered the pouting lips between her thighs. She was, Slocum thought, one of the great beauties, from her hair down to the delicate shape of her feet.

She was staring at his fierce flesh, swollen big with longing.

He led her to the bed, lay her down, then bent to her pink-nippled breasts with his lips and tongue. She lay like a statue, as if amazed at her feelings. His hands caressed her breasts, her belly, her thighs. He looked at the pink pouting lips and, caught by a gust of passion, he leaned to her, kissing and caressing her there. The sensations seemed to delight her.

He brought her hand to his hard flesh; it sent a shudder through her and she held him so tightly it almost hurt.

He bent to kiss her, slid over her body, and her thighs went apart instinctively. He brought himself between her thighs, pushed gently into her, and felt the smooth velvet moist warmth.

Slowly he pushed in, feeling the flesh part. She was tight but open, and he pleasured in the sensations.

He thrust gently, piercing her, feeling his length finally sink into her body; he was entirely within her.

"Oh," she breathed.

Her body was enchanted by his flesh, he could tell.

He began his moves, gently at the beginning, building up rhythm, and she soon picked it up, her body responding with instinctive appetite.

His movements after a time became more and more fierce, and her arms tightened about his body. The pleasure of possessing her was so intense that his excitement could no longer be controlled and, in sudden movements, he thrust and thrust as he felt her own excitement mount. Then he felt the anguish of passion at its climax. Her body, too, went into a frenzy of movement, and she flung herself against him, as if intolerable magic was happening in her body.

They were suspended in a rare moment of pleasure. Then they dropped limply to the bed, as if in exhaustion.

When the fog cleared away for her and he moved, she said, "Where are you going, Slocum?"

He thought carefully.

"Nowhere for quite a time, Cassie. A man would be crazy to walk away from this in a hurry."

She smiled brilliantly.

"In that case, let's try this thing again, Slocum. You seem to be very good with pistols."

GREAT WESTERN YARNS FROM ONE OF THE BEST-SELLING WRITERS IN THE FIELD TODAY

JAKE LOGAN

Prices may be slightly higher in Canada.

JAKE LOGAN

J.D. HARDIN

"THE MOST EXCITING
WESTERN WRITER SINCE
LOUIS L'AMOUR"
—JAKE LOGAN

___ 872-16869-7	THE SPIRIT AND THE FLESH	$1.95
___ 867-21226-8	BOBBIES, BAUBLES AND BLOOD	$2.25
___ 06572-3	DEATH LODE	$2.25
___ 06410-7	DOWNRIVER TO HELL	$2.25
___ 06001-2	BIBLES, BULLETS AND BRIDES	$2.25
___ 06331-3	BLOODY TIME IN BLACKTOWER	$2.25
___ 06248-1	HANGMAN'S NOOSE	$2.25
___ 06337-2	THE MAN WITH NO FACE	$2.25
___ 06151-5	SASKATCHEWAN RISING	$2.25
___ 06412-3	BOUNTY HUNTER	$2.50
___ 06743-2	QUEENS OVER DEUCES	$2.50
___ 07017-4	LEAD-LINED COFFINS	$2.50
___ 08013-7	THE WYOMING SPECIAL	$2.50
___ 07259-2	THE PECOS DOLLARS	$2.50
___ 07257-6	SAN JUAN SHOOTOUT	$2.50
___ 07379-3	OUTLAW TRAIL	$2.50
___ 07392-0	THE OZARK OUTLAWS	$2.50
___ 07461-7	TOMBSTONE IN DEADWOOD	$2.50
___ 07381-5	HOMESTEADER'S REVENGE	$2.50
___ 07386-6	COLORADO SILVER QUEEN	$2.50
___ 07790-X	THE BUFFALO SOLDIER	$2.50
___ 07785-3	THE GREAT JEWEL ROBBERY	$2.50
___ 07789-6	THE COCHISE COUNTY WAR	$2.50
___ 07974-0	THE COLORADO STING	$2.50
___ 08032-3	HELL'S BELLE	$2.50
___ 08088-9	THE CATTLETOWN WAR	$2.50
___ 08190-7	THE GHOST MINE	$2.50
___ 08280-6	MAXIMILIAN'S GOLD	$2.50
___ 08669-0	THE TINCUP RAILROAD WAR	$2.50

Prices may be slightly higher in Canada.